Nig...

KATHE... GARBERA

*First published in Great Britain 2007
by Harlequin Mills & Boon Limited,
Eton House, 18-24 Paradise Road, Richmond, Surrey TW9 1SR*

© Katherine Garbera 2004

ISBN: 978 0 263 85776 4

46-1207

*Harlequin Mills & Boon policy is to use papers that are
natural, renewable and recyclable products and made from
wood grown in sustainable forests. The logging and
manufacturing processes conform to the legal environmental
regulations of the country of origin.*

*Printed and bound in Spain
by Litografía Rosés S.A., Barcelona*

KATHERINE GARBERA

is an award-winning, bestselling author. Garbera started making up stories for her own benefit when she was on a competitive swimming team at school. Though she went to Florida State and did well, Katherine says her heart wasn't in swimming but rather in the stories she created as she swam laps at practice. Katherine holds a red belt in the martial art of Tae Kwon Do and vows that there's not a piece of plywood out there that can take her in a fair match! Readers can visit her on the web at katherinegarbera.com.

In loving memory of Priscilla Tromblay, my paternal grandmother, who lived life on her own terms with a fierce and independent spirit. Thanks for showing me that anything can be accomplished if you work hard enough at it.

Acknowledgements:

Thanks to Rob Elser for answering my many questions about life in London and the UK.

Thanks to Janet Justiss for helping me with the French dialogue – any mistakes are my own!

Thanks to Mary Louise Wells for helping with the initial polish of the proposal; Eve Gaddy for just always being there when I called; and Beverly Brandt for her helpful advice on writing a bigger story.

As always, thanks to my family, who are always supportive of whatever idea I have.

Prologue

> The fact that our task is exactly as large as our
> life makes it infinite.
>
> —Franz Kafka

The wind shifted to blow from the north but no sound emerged from the surrounding woods. The silence was unnatural. Nightshade tensed, every sense on hyperalert.

Nothing was hidden from her vantage point. In the clearing near the chopper was a puddle of darkness. It could just be shadows from the clouds covering the moon, but she sensed a human presence there.

Townsend. As smart as he was lethal, Elias Townsend had once been a master spy for Her Majesty's

Intelligence Agency. Frustrated with agency bureaucracy, he'd crossed over to the life of a criminal and never looked back. A tall, thin man with a wiry build, Townsend was a challenging adversary.

Her father had taught her to respect the enemy. Because when you got cocky you got dead. Nightshade didn't want to die—she was still young and had too much to live for. Her old man had learned that security was an illusion and had raised Nightshade to protect both herself and those weaker than she was.

Except she'd done a piss-poor job of saving her childhood pal, Senator Ellingham's son, Perry. At least she had evened the score by killing Townsend's right-hand man.

She shut out everything, narrowing her focus to that dark shadow. She waited. The Glock .9 mm automatic felt like a natural extension of her arm. And then he moved, quickly and jerkily. She'd hit him earlier in their exchange of gunfire. She sprang to her feet, a lethal predator sprinting to intercept Townsend.

He pivoted as she approached, leveling his own gun at her. Still in motion, Nightshade leaped in the air and used a forward kick to hit him solidly in the shoulder. A gunshot exploded and she felt the bullet graze her thigh. She cataloged the surface wound and promised herself she'd worry about it later. It wasn't enough to stop her as she brought all her weight down on him. His head bounced against the concrete of the landing pad.

Nightshade twisted her heel in Townsend's shoulder until he cried out and his fingers opened, releasing his weapon. Keeping her gun trained on him, she stooped and picked up his weapon, tucking it into the back of her waistband.

Leveling the Glock at him, she watched him squirm. Killing had never really been a part of the job she liked. In fact, it was the one thing she genuinely hated. But sometimes, the mission called for it.

This time, she wanted justice for Perry's death. She wanted to exact the kind of eye-for-an-eye retribution that her father had always advocated.

She knelt beside Townsend and pressed the barrel of the Glock against his temple. A rage swam through her body, blinding her to everything except the desire to kill. Every instinct she had screamed for her to pull the trigger. Her finger trembled and she started to squeeze.

Sweat beaded Townsend's forehead and he shivered under her foot. She pressed the barrel harder against his skin. It would be so easy—and so hard.

"Kill me already if you're going to."

She almost listened to him, but at the last moment eased her finger from the trigger before her emotions could get the better of her. Killing Townsend now— like this—would make her little better than he was.

He rolled toward her, knocking her on her ass. And the tables were turned. He towered over her, a six-inch switchblade in his hand.

She fired at his shoulder. Blood spurted and ran down his hand, but he didn't drop his weapon. She scrambled to her feet as he advanced on her, never taking her gaze from his menacing figure.

Townsend watched her with cold eyes and she knew she'd made a stupid, rookie mistake in not cuffing him when she'd had the chance. Her orders were to bring him in alive. She holstered her gun.

He feinted to the left and then attacked her with a swipe of his knife. She dodged the blow easily and countered with a front jab that connected solidly with his jaw. His head snapped back and he growled at her. And then he surprised her with a roundhouse kick to the chest. She was stunned momentarily but quickly recovered as he sprinted for the chopper.

Concentrating all her energy on ignoring the throbbing pain in her thigh, she ran after him, hitting him with a powerful kick to the side. He fell in a broken heap. His head impacted with the solid ground again. He moaned with pain. Nightshade landed with one foot on his wrist, pinning him to the ground. She stooped, grabbed his wrist and twisted it behind his back, bringing his other hand to join it. She cuffed his hands together with a zip cord and stood.

She keyed the small radio mike attached to her collar and asked for a pickup. She watched Townsend carefully; he was much too quiet to be trusted. She heard the far-off sound of a crying baby.

She scanned the landing pad. A child? The cries grew louder and louder. What the hell?

Chapter 1

Not everyone can see the truth, but everyone can be the truth.

—Franz Kafka

Sasha Malone-Sterling sat up in bed. The scar from the 5-year-old gunshot wound on her thigh throbbed. She reached for the pillow next to hers—empty. She rolled away from that side of the bed.

No wonder she'd been dreaming again. It was the only outlet she had for excitement. At least it wasn't one of her more erotic dreams about the time when she and Kane had been lovers. She rubbed her eyes. No, those dreams only plagued her when he was lying beside her in bed. Physically close but emotionally miles away.

She glanced at the clock next to the bed: 3:00 a.m. The television baby monitor on the nightstand showed her eighteen-month-old son, Dylan, standing in his crib crying.

She rolled out of bed and made her way to her son's room. She didn't bother with a robe. Wearing only the black silk long underwear she slept in, she made her way quickly down the hall.

Entering the room, she scanned the shadows for anything untoward but found only her son crying. She scooped Dylan up and cradled him to her chest, dropping butterfly kisses on his head. "Mommy's here."

He snuggled closer to her, rubbing his tear-stained face against her shoulder. His little arms came up to encircle her neck, holding her with a fierceness that she cherished. "Mama."

She rubbed his back and rocked side to side, soothing her son, whose heart raced. This wasn't the first time she'd been awakened from a dream of her former life by her son's cries. She hoped he hadn't picked up her tension.

Up until her pregnancy, she'd worked for American Renegade Company. They were an elite task force comprising operatives who worked hand in hand with the American government in overseas operations. Their agents were all from very wealthy backgrounds and for the most part led double lives.

Now she was a wife and mother in Leeds, England. Talk about culture shock.

The door leading from the nanny's room opened. Though Dylan didn't have an ordinary nanny. She'd hired a bodyguard for her son. She could protect Dylan and would with her life, but she knew that there would be times when having someone at her back would be invaluable.

Sasha pivoted to face the man entering. Orly was late. His response time had been much quicker when they'd worked in the field. But these days they were a step above rent-a-cops, doing routine security set-ups for domestic businesses.

Orly LaFontaine, the man who'd been her partner for years with the Agency, stumbled into the room. Orly wasn't your typical bodyguard, and he hadn't been your typical agent either. Sasha had saved his life in Nigeria and Orly had never forgotten it. He believed deeply that a life saved is a life earned and had dedicated himself to repaying Sasha.

He'd traded a life of intrigue to join her in this suburban house, leaving behind his trendy London flat and his women. Though his appearance tonight negated that.

His short blond hair was spiked up with blue highlights. Usually he dressed in clothes more suited to the punk rockers he'd grown up with than the business crowd they mixed with, but tonight he wore only a pair of brief boxers and lipstick smudges on his neck.

"Bloody hell, Sasha. I'm sorry," Orly said. His accent was a rough Cockney that he let few people hear. Most people who met him believed him to be some sort of aristocratic Englishman by birth and breeding. He was a master chameleon.

Seeing her old friend pushed away the last vestiges of the tension lingering from her dream. "No problem. Looks like you're having more fun in bed than I was."

Orly crossed to her and patted Dylan's head. Her son had calmed completely and was now resting peacefully in Sasha's arms. Sometimes she wished she'd been attracted to Orly the way she was with Kane. It would have made life so much easier.

Kane was an agent for Her Majesty's Intelligence Agency. Similar in scope to MI-6, they were a more elite team who went deep undercover, targeting enemies of the Crown. They'd met while working on a mission together four years ago.

"Sasha?"

"Sorry. I've got D. You can go back to her." Orly suspected that Kane had moved out, but until Sasha confirmed it, he'd keep his questions to himself. Which was what she needed. Kane felt that she'd turned into a zombie since Dylan's birth and she couldn't argue that without Kane realizing her emotional distance had actually started earlier.

Orly watched her carefully with perceptive green eyes that missed no detail.

He said nothing until she'd placed Dylan in his crib. Sasha grabbed the soft fluffy panda from the bottom of the crib and tucked it next to her son. His arm tightened around the plush animal.

"He looks like you when you crash."

"He's drooling, Orly."

"Hey, boss lady, I hate to tell you this, but underneath that beautiful face, you've got some nasty habits."

She punched his shoulder and he laughed. Orly was one of the few people she really trusted. She knew his secrets and he knew hers. There was balance in their relationship, unlike her marriage to Kane, which was…not. She had no one to blame but herself.

"You okay?" he asked.

She crossed to the window. The night sky was clear and the half moon cast long shadows on the landscaped lawn. A breeze blew and the trees swayed lightly with it, their shadows moving across the lawn. "I'm restless."

Orly moved to stand next to her, dropping his arm across her shoulders. "I wanna say—hot damn, this is a good thing but you don't sound happy about this."

"I have a son now."

"Do you want me to find something more exciting than installing a security system for a bed-and-breakfast?"

She shrugged. She could justify many things in her mind, but endangering her son she couldn't do. And she couldn't be an agent and be a mother. She didn't have an on-off switch that she could toggle from protective nurturer to avenger. "Not yet."

She wanted to go back to her old job. But then she'd have to really find a nanny for Dylan and another bodyguard, because Orly would be with her. And she couldn't do that. Not yet. Maybe once Dylan started school. God, what a mess. She who'd vowed to never put her life on hold for any man was torn because of two. One she'd loved too much to keep, and the other—she glanced over at her sleeping son—the other was her entire life.

A subtle beep emitted from the pager on Dylan's dresser. *Intruder.* She crossed the room to the *Monet Seashore* painting and swung it to the left. A quick glance at the crib showed Dylan across the room, sleeping undisturbed. The lighted monitor indicated someone moving from the kitchen toward the west wing and the bedrooms.

God, it had been so long since they'd had to deal with anything like this. She wished Kane were home. Orly was good but he wasn't Kane. And when your home was being invaded, you wanted your husband around.

"Is that your girl?" Sasha asked.

"Uh, no. She's tied to the bed."

"Go untie her and take Dylan with you. Hole up until I give you the signal."

"What are you going to be doing?" he asked. She knew that he didn't care for this any more than she did. If there was one thing she knew about her partner, it was that he hated hiding out as much as she did. But only one of them was needed to neutralize their visitor and she was the senior partner.

"Taking care of our intruder."

"You don't have a weapon," he said.

"I'll get one."

Sasha moved silently through the house. She'd swung by her bedroom to remove the 9 mm Glock that fit her hand as if it was made for her. She wondered if her past had finally caught up with her, and felt more than a moment's fear that she wouldn't be able to rise to the task. Sure, she had a lifetime of training, but lately the most exciting thing she'd done was organizing a playdate with a group of moms from her neighborhood.

She trusted Kane and his security measures to protect their son. Forgetting that Nightshade had more enemies than most agents and that her husband had become a man she didn't really know anymore.

She tucked the Glock into the holster at the small of her back. The intruder moved quickly and Sasha moved back into the shadows, waiting for him to pass her position. As soon as he did, she attacked him from behind with a side kick that connected solidly to his midsection. He countered with a sweeping roundhouse kick that caught her shoulder. Sasha stepped to the left and countered with a back-kick, front-jab combo that pushed her assailant up against the wall.

Family pictures rattled under the impact but the intruder paused, facing her. His eyes were the color of the ocean on a stormy day, though she couldn't see them clearly in this light. Husky in build and slightly over six feet tall. In fact, he reminded her a bit of…

"Dammit, girl. Can't a father visit his only child without it turning into a sparring match? You're rusty, by the way," her dad growled. Sergeant Major Mitch Malone pulled her close for a bear hug. Her old man smelled of Cuban cigars, which were the only ones he smoked. He always said that damn embargo was a foolish, political waste of time.

"Most fathers ring the doorbell. Besides, I'm retired, I'm entitled to be rusty."

"Didn't want to wake my grandson," he said. He was dressed in battle fatigues and combat boots. He was armed as well with the same Colt .45 he'd carried since she'd been born.

"How'd you get here?" she asked, leading him down the hall to the kitchen.

"Military transport via Germany."

Sasha was breathing hard and struggling not to show it. She closed her eyes for a moment as relief swamped her. She'd held her own. She wasn't as out of shape as she'd feared she might be. She also felt that seductive rush of adrenaline that only came from facing an enemy and outsmarting him. Her father moved into the room as if he was on a recon mission.

The kitchen was big and airy and filled with shadows. She scanned the space before turning on the lights.

This didn't bode well. She hit the intercom switch and informed Orly that the intruder had been neutralized and that the sergeant major was in the house.

"Who says I've been neutralized?" her dad asked.

She gave her dad a wry glance. Her father had more gray in his hair now, but otherwise he still was the toughest-looking man she'd ever seen. "I do."

He shrugged and said in that smart-ass way of his, "I'd call it a stalemate. You weren't exactly kicking my butt."

She didn't want to discuss her own failings. Taking her time getting back into shape since giving birth to Dylan had made sense. Motherhood was her chief focus now.

But the old man was right. She'd been slow and sloppy tonight; if anyone other than her dad had broken in she'd have been in big trouble.

Instead of dwelling on that, she said, "Why are you here?"

"You need to come out of retirement."

"We've been over this before. I'm a wife and mother now." Even though Kane had argued that she was too young to retire, Sasha had stood firm. She was also not sure she could keep everything balanced. Being a mom was tougher than she'd thought it would be.

"Kane needs you."

Blood rushed in her ears and she had to sit down. Kane hadn't really needed her. That's one of the reasons he'd left. "What do you mean?"

No matter how she felt about her relationship, she wasn't ready to give up on it. Though things were strained between the two of them, neither of them had left.

"Townsend has surfaced again and he's up to his old tricks with HMIA."

"I'm sure Kane will catch Townsend. He's one of Her Majesty's best men."

"Not anymore."

"Dad, stop talking in circles. What are you trying to say?"

"Hold up a sec then I'll tell you."

Pulling a small wandlike device from his back pocket, her father made a slow sweep of the room. She rolled her eyes as she watched him work. Sasha and Orly swept for bugs routinely. Her father took paranoia to new extremes. There were no bugs in her house as of three days ago.

She took no chances with the safety of this house, especially now that Kane had moved back to London. Security was one of the things she knew how to provide and she'd made their little house into a fortress to protect Dylan.

She boiled water for coffee and scooped some grounds into her French press. Orly entered the room as her father neared the third wall. He didn't glance up from his task. Orly turned around one of the ladder-back chairs at the table and sat down.

"What's he looking for?" Orly asked as Sasha set a cup of coffee in front of him.

"Bugs."

Orly raised one eyebrow at her. Sasha shrugged. Orly had met her dad before in the States and had even visited his remote home in the mountains of Georgia, so watching her father in action wasn't really shocking. "Sergeant Major, don't you trust me to protect your daughter and grandson? This is what I do."

"I don't really trust anyone," he said, focusing on the phone.

She'd never talk about her past life on the phone. In fact, she had few friends from the old days. Still, it begged the question as to why her dad thought someone was listening in on her conversations. She had a sinking feeling in her gut that had saved her ass many times in the old days. That feeling that said everything was about to break around her.

"Do you really believe that someone is fishing around for information?" Orly said.

Her dad nodded.

Sasha shivered and checked the baby monitor affixed to the kitchen counter. *What was going on?*

Dylan was safely tucked away in his crib. She wanted to go to the security room and ramp up all their alarms. Let her dad sweep the entire house.

"It's not Sasha's secrets I'm worried about," her father said.

She started running scenarios in her head. But before she went off half-cocked, she looked at the man who'd brought this to her door. "Maybe you'd better tell me why you're here, Dad."

The dainty china mug looked like a toy in his big hands. It reminded her of the tea parties she'd had as a little girl. Her father hadn't wanted her to grow up with too much male influence. So he'd encouraged Sasha to have tea parties and wear pink, a color she'd never really liked. Still, she'd admired her dad for trying to give her a rounded upbringing without having her mom in the picture.

He gave her a stern look. And her stomach sank. "Kane has gone rogue. He's taken the STAR list and is out in the open. I talked to Ano at American Renegade Company and she's reinstated you as an agent for the duration of this mission."

The STAR list contained the codenames and current locations of every known operative. Not just for HMIA, but for many of the intelligence agencies around the world.

Sasha felt a cold chill down her back. Why would Kane go rogue? The last six months had been tense, which was why he'd left her and moved back to London. But this was extreme for him. He was one of the most secure and well balanced people she knew.

Ano aka Alpha Number One was the head of American Renegade Company. Sasha didn't know all the details, but Ano and the sergeant major had some sort of ongoing relationship. They couldn't live together and yet living apart wasn't what they wanted either.

She pushed away from the table and paced to the window. Her dad had worked for Renegade Company for years. *Renegade* wasn't just a cute catchphrase they used. They were a group of renegades that no other law-enforcement group would have. "If I don't accept this assignment, someone else will, right?"

She heard his chair scrape against the tile floor as he stood. In the window she saw him come up behind her. He didn't put his arm around her, but stood just behind her. "Ano wants it to be you. HMIA doesn't want you anywhere near this because of potential conflict of interest."

She pivoted to face him. Conflict of interest didn't even come close. Good God, she didn't want to get between Kane and his target. "Why does Ano want me? She knows I've gone against the Company before. I've been out there like Kane."

Her dad lifted his hand toward her shoulder, but he dropped it before he touched her. She'd alienated him as well. That last mission had almost killed her, not physically but emotionally. Her soul was empty except for Dylan, and all the men in her life had felt the chill.

"That's why, Sasha. You came back and she thinks you can talk Kane into it. If you can't, they're going to sanction him."

She hadn't exactly made it all the way back and they both knew it. Relieved that her father didn't call her on it, she said, "Tell me the details."

"Ano will brief you. All I know is that Townsend is in London and that Kane is stalking him."

"What does Townsend have?" Sasha asked. Her enemy had escaped the authorities by killing one of his guards and knocking the other unconscious.

Her father looked down at his coffee and took a swallow before responding. "We think at least one hostage."

It wasn't like her old man to stall. What did he know that he wasn't saying?

"And negotiation isn't an option?" she asked. But she knew it wasn't. Townsend's mode of operation was to take the family members of influential people and use them as pawns in his deadly games.

Sasha felt a deep rage start burning inside. And clenched her fists against the feelings sweeping through her. If she gave in to the rage, she'd never be able to get the job done.

"He'll probably try to get his hostages out of Britain," she said. Townsend knew how HMIA worked. Hell, he'd written half of the procedures they used for this kind of thing.

Orly's eyes had taken on a glazed look that she knew meant he was processing the information. His mind was like a computer.

"I'm going to run some information through my computer. What time are we leaving?" Orly asked.

"Ano is expecting you by six," Mitch said.

"Meet me out front in about an hour."

Orly left the room and Sasha faced her father. He didn't look happy delivering that news. No matter what he thought of her marriage to Kane, her dad had always respected her husband because of his attitude toward the world and his willingness to make many sacrifices to keep it safe.

Kane gone rogue. Why? It didn't make sense. He was a loyal agent and one of the most balanced men she'd ever met. He was cool under fire, and in the field she'd never met his match. She crossed her arms over her chest and rubbed her hands up and down trying to get warm. She'd made a choice and cut herself off from Kane. Was she responsible for this action?

Was this some bid for her attention? One he knew she wouldn't be able to resist?

Why would he do it? She and Dylan were safe. His mother and two sisters were safe, Sasha had talked to her mother-in-law, Jane, two days ago. There was no one close to Kane who could be in danger. Was it Bruce Temple, Kane's partner? She rubbed her eyes. God, what a mess.

"Orly's gone. You can tell me everything."

Her old man shrugged and had that stubborn look in his eyes. He wouldn't reveal his sources to anyone. Not even his daughter. Sasha often wondered if that was why she had such a hard time trusting men.

"Do you know why Kane's doing this?"

"I couldn't get that intel. Ano either didn't know or wouldn't tell me."

"The threat is real, Sasha. Get Kane and get the information he has—now, before it falls into the wrong hands."

Her heart lurched and she gave up questioning her father and started planning. She calculated the time it would take to change clothes, ready the command vehicle and get to London.

She'd find Townsend and finish the job this time. She wasn't going to let him take the life of another man she cared about.

She trusted her dad to protect Dylan. She watched the old man for a minute. His credo was, protect those who couldn't protect themselves. "Dad, you stay here and keep Dylan safe."

"I planned to."

Sasha walked slowly down the hallway and back to Dylan's room. He was sleeping quietly now, his arm wrapped around that panda of his. He looked sweet, innocent and just enough like Kane to make her heart break. Neither she nor Kane were innocent, but they'd vowed to protect the world so that more people could be. What had happened to radically change Kane?

Ano hadn't changed in the year since Sasha had seen her boss. Ano moved into the room as if she owned it. She was a tall woman, almost six feet, and her brilliant auburn hair was pulled back in a sleek-looking ponytail. Her eyes radiated the kind of quiet intelligence that Sasha respected. Sasha and Orly had made good time in the Aston Martin that Kane had given her as a wedding present.

A.R.C. headquarters was located in the Trafalgar Square section of London. Trendy nightclubs surrounded them. Sasha couldn't have felt more out of place if she'd tried. This was a world away from her quiet life of playing in the park with Dylan and talking to B and B owners about room security.

This was the game she'd left behind before it chewed her up anymore and spit her out. Sasha felt an odd sense of déjà vu. She'd never expected to be here again. Reconciling the conflicting emotions wasn't easy.

"Nightshade, it's good to see you," Ano said. She gestured for Sasha to take a seat in one of the brocade guest chairs.

But was it good for her? Sasha wondered. She was a mother now, a wife. In the old days she'd never left the house without her gun, her GPS unit and her two-way radio. These days she never left without baby wipes, a pacifier and a plastic container of Cheerios. "Thanks, Ano. I'm not exactly happy to be here."

"Given the circumstances, I understand." There was compassion and a bit of doubt in Ano's eyes.

Sasha took the compassion and ignored the doubt. She had her own trepidation about taking on this assignment. But overriding that gut reaction was the reality that she wouldn't let anyone else go after Kane.

"Your mission is to retrieve Agent Sterling and do some recon on Townsend to identify his location."

Her gut tightened at the thought of retrieving Kane. She still had so many questions.

"Why is Kane out there?"

"Our intel didn't say. Only that he took the STAR list."

Sasha inhaled sharply. That list was an extensive database that was used by all global intelligence agencies. It held the location of all the safe houses the agencies used and a list of code words. If the list were compromised, there would be no way to warn all the agents in the field until it was too late. Kane held the lives of agents all over the world in his hands. No wonder he was wanted back. "Why?"

"Townsend wants it in return for the hostages he's holding."

"Kane wouldn't—"

"Forget about your husband, Nightshade. This is a rogue agent. Sterling needs to be brought in. Is it going to be you or should I send someone else?"

Ano didn't pull her punches but then Sasha hadn't expected her to. Sasha closed her eyes and searched inside herself. The world disappeared and she found the quiet place that she always visited before a mission.

Each time it was the same, she realized. Her doubts and fears weren't new; she'd always questioned if she was ready to go out and face an enemy who was willing to kill her to achieve his objective. And this time she knew with utter certainty that she was the only agent who had a stake in keeping Kane alive.

"I'm the agent for this job," she said quietly.

Ano didn't say anything, but steepled her fingers and watched Sasha. Sasha had no idea what Ano was hoping to find in her expression, but when Ano nodded Sasha knew she'd found it.

Ano passed her a manila folder. She opened it and skimmed the contents. Kane had walked out of HMIA's headquarters twenty-four hours ago, leaving behind his shield and agency-issued guy. He'd taken the STAR list on a microchip and knocked out three guards.

His current position wasn't known, but American Renegade Company had a lead from one of their sources that indicated Kane was headed to Southampton, a port town south of London.

"I'll start in Southampton," Nightshade said.

"Agreed. I've got Charity and Justice down there now. They haven't been able to pick up his trail."

"I can."

Ano smiled for the first time since Nightshade had entered the room. "I know. What do you need?"

"Access to your databases and satellites."

"Weapons or backup?"

"Dad packed my weapons bag. I've got handguns, rifles and probably a few other surprises. Orly's the only backup I need."

"Nightshade?"

Sasha glanced back over her shoulder. "I brought this to you because you are the only one who can do it."

Sasha nodded and walked out the door. She knew that deep inside her seethed a kind of darkness that had been waiting a long time to get out again.

She and Orly were just south of London near the docks at Southampton. The area comprised mainly warehouses and berths for large shipping vessels. Nightshade left Orly behind in their mobile computer-information center and headed for the warehouse where she'd determined Kane would be. Charity and Justice were working the town, talking to contacts and trying to find a lead.

It had been a long day of fruitless searches, and Nightshade realized that she'd forgotten the tediousness of undercover work. It was 2100 hours and she was glad to finally have a solid lead. A man matching Kane's description had been seen in a tavern in this area earlier today.

She'd called her dad a few minutes ago and sung Dylan his bedtime song—"Mockingbird". His sweet little voice babbling nonsense words had calmed her. And had made her more determined to find **Kane**.

Damn the man, he was a father. He couldn't take these kinds of risks anymore.

Now she left behind the last traces of Sasha and transformed herself into Nightshade. She focused on the transition, letting all her senses grow more attuned to the night. The air was cool and brisk on this April evening, and if it weren't for the possible loss of her husband, she would have relished being back at work.

The alley behind the Ramman Brothers warehouse reeked of trash, rotting fish and, unless she was mistaken, some kind of excrement. Ah, the glamorous life of an operative. Nightshade adjusted her shoulder holster and scanned the area.

Kane might not be too happy to see Nightshade again. It wouldn't be the first time she'd rescued him. Not that he hadn't saved her ass a time or two. They'd worked well as a team. Both sensing each other's reactions and playing off each other's strengths.

Sasha had forgotten all about those days. Well, not exactly forgotten—she'd suppressed those memories.

Just the thought of Kane in trouble was enough to enrage her, but she bottled up those feelings for later. She slipped past the Dumpster and decaying fire-escape stairs into clear view. No one was in the alley.

Dammit, Kane. What was he thinking? She was being slowly drawn back into the life she'd given up. And she began to understand why she'd been afraid to come back. She might not be able to leave it behind again.

She scanned the area one more time. Townsend didn't play around. If he wanted that list, he wouldn't stop until he got it. Why was he suddenly going after it now?

In the past he'd been one of the most successful smugglers in Europe. When he decided to grab a hostage and move, he did it quickly.

There were large metal storage tanks littering the dock and Sasha searched for a lorry—a big eighteen-wheeler or an animal-cargo vehicle. That was the common way to smuggle people in and out of the country.

"I'm going in," she whispered into her voice-activated wireless communicator. Orly was down the street waiting for her in the refitted Land Rover they'd always used on missions. She hadn't been surprised when Orly revealed he'd kept everything up to date in there.

"Gotcha. Satellite shows three bodies just inside the warehouse. There are two sentries patrolling near the docks on each end of the building," Orly said.

"Direct me in."

Orly whispered directions in her ear and she moved carefully through the area, visually searching for Kane.

She drew her Glock. A shiver danced down her spine the way it always did when she pulled her weapon.

"Let my aim be accurate and deadly," she murmured to herself. Though she'd been easing back into her physical regimen of exercise, she'd never stopped practicing with the Glock for two hours every day. She hadn't wanted to lose her marksmanship.

She neared the rear entrance to the building, picked the lock in short order then oiled the hinges on the weathered door before opening it. "I'm at the south-side entrance. Where's the sentry?"

"Opposite corner."

Slowly, she opened the door. The dim bulb provided scant illumination in the corridor. "I'm in. Do you have me on your screen?"

"Gotcha. There's no one moving near you."

"Gotcha," she said, taking a few moments to oil the hinges on a second door before carefully opening it. It opened without a sound and Nightshade slipped quickly into the total darkness of the room beyond.

Damn. She didn't want to use a penlight. She had a pair of night-vision goggles in her pack and put them on quickly.

"I've lost you on satellite," Orly said.

"I'm in. This floor looks like mainly office space. Did you access the blueprint for the building?"

"The only one on file is from 1977. Heads up. The figure on the stairwell has moved past your floor."

She acknowledged Orly and then paused to scan the area around the door and move slowly into the room quartering it. Everything was coming back to her. Old instincts coming to the fore; it was like putting on a comfortable pair of jeans. She'd missed the feel of this, she realized.

Sasha stopped and considered Kane and the way

he worked. This is what he had wanted her to do. Ironically he'd gotten his wish. They were in the field together.

She knew where he'd be. Whatever location had the best advantage for watching the dock. And that would be the northeast corner of the building.

There were a ring of offices against the walls and an open area in the center. She checked the center area first and found nothing.

Starting at the back, she worked her way from office to office, carefully opening each door and scanning each room for any signs of life. She kept Orly posted so they'd have a fairly accurate report of what was on this floor. Empty offices with desks but no sign of Kane.

Was she in the wrong place? She pushed those thoughts to the back of her mind, focusing instead on the darkened office. The next two offices had closed doors. She checked the hinges first; they were new-looking and not rusty.

She turned the first handle and pushed gently, but the lock was jammed. She put her shoulder to the door and forced it open. Stepping into the room, she found the window open a crack. Just large enough for the barrel of a rifle.

"I think I've found something," she muttered.

"Are you alone?"

She scanned the interior of the room. "Yes. But someone's been here recently."

"Nightshade, that's a negative. Someone is still there."

Before she could move, a man stepped out from behind the file cabinet and grabbed her. He shoved the barrel of a gun up under her chin, forcing her head back.

Chapter 2

To the mind that is still the whole universe surrenders.

—Lao-tzu

Sasha leaned back against Kane. He was wearing body armor. And holding an Enfield SA80 battle rifle loosely in his free hand, the muzzle of his Heckler & Koch USP MK23 pressed against her skin.

By turning her head she could see that he had on a night-vision mask and a scope on his rifle. Her blood turned cold. Kane wasn't a sniper. But for some reason he was tonight. She had a million questions and really no time to ask them. She knew only that she had to get Kane out of here before he destroyed a career he'd spent over fifteen years creating.

And she also knew from her own walk on the outside of the Company that vengeance was never worth the price. He had gone rogue. What if she couldn't get him to back down? She knew she'd never be able to kill him but that someone else wouldn't hesitate.

She leaned against his chest and tipped her head backward. Taking a deep breath, she pushed aside all her doubts. She had a job to do and that job, quite frankly, was to stop Kane from leaking sensitive information and blowing the operation in place for rescuing the hostages.

"Hello, lover," she said. Her soft, naturally husky voice pitched low enough not to carry on the wind. His scent was familiar to her and she closed her eyes, breathing deeply for a minute.

He cursed softly under his breath and released her. "Go home, Sasha."

He moved away from her back to the window and positioned his rifle on the ledge. She slid into position beside him. "Nightshade."

This time he looked at her. Even in the shadows she felt the intensity of his gaze on her. She stood a little taller—he'd always had that effect on her. She didn't know why this one man should make her want to preen and show off, but he did.

"What are you doing here?" he asked in a low voice that carried no farther than her ears. He took a few moments to holster his sidearm and then she heard a click. Kane wore a thick black Irish sweater and a pair of dark chinos.

He looked like Cary Grant in *To Catch A Thief.* Her

heartbeat picked up and she was reminded of how sexy her husband could be when he wasn't playing the English lord of the manor. God, she'd missed him.

"I heard you needed some backup," she said softly.

"Is that all you heard?" he asked.

"No. I couldn't let you do something stupid," she said, not caring if he got angry with her. The risks he was taking were stupid.

He shook his head. "You know better than that."

"I only know that HMIA is sending someone to bring you in because you have some sensitive information. That doesn't sound smart to me."

"I know what I'm doing."

"Sure you do. That's why you're alone in a warehouse about to betray your country and your peers."

"I don't have time for this. Go home."

"Come with me," she said. *Please come with me.* She willed him to morph back into the man she'd married, not this steely-eyed assassin.

She'd sparred with Kane a number of times. She knew his weaknesses as well as he knew hers. Or at least as well as he knew the ones she'd let him see.

"Why'd they send you? I was expecting Temple."

Sasha figured HMIA would send Kane's partner as well. And then either Kane or Temple would end up dead. And there was something in Kane's manner tonight that she'd never seen before. Something that warned her that he wasn't going to back down easily.

She knew there had to be more to the situation

than she had been informed of. "Are you having a problem at work?"

Kane gave a short derisive laugh. "That's an understatement."

"Help me understand this, Kane."

"There's nothing for a housewife to understand," he said.

She knew he was goading her. And suspected it was because he wanted her out of here. "I'm not leaving until I get some answers. Why did you take the STAR list?"

"Stop the chitchat, Nightshade," Orly said. "There is some activity on the dock. A BMW with dark windows just pulled up. If you don't get Kane out of there now, it'll be too late."

"Gotcha, Orly."

Kane's eyes narrowed as Sasha spoke. "Who's watching Dylan?"

"Dad."

There was some movement on the dock and Kane crouched down and sighted his rifle, and she heard the minute sound of a bullet being pushed through a silencer. The man whom Kane had aimed at crumpled to the dock.

"How many men are you going to kill?" she asked softly. The man she'd married always avoided killing suspects, usually just wounding them. This wasn't the Kane she knew. And that scared her.

"As many as I have to." His voice was devoid of any emotion and she knew he was in work mode.

"Why are you here, Kane? Help me understand."

"Not now, Sasha. I'm on a tight clock. Go home."

He panned the scope, carefully searching for others on the dock. Then he stood, lifted the window and gave her a half salute before stepping over the edge.

Dammit, that was what that click was. Only now did she notice the harness and the rappelling rope. He went down smoothly and quickly. Sasha grabbed the rope and followed Kane over the edge. By the time she was on the ground, he'd moved off, blending into the shadows.

He reached the man he'd taken down and dragged the body out of the walkway. Nightshade kept her distance, waiting for the right moment to make her move. She was going to have to take him down.

"Three men are headed toward your position," Orly told her.

Nightshade glanced toward the warehouse and made visual contact. "I see them. Kane, we got company."

They were probably coming to investigate what had happened to the guy Kane just shot. Kane lifted his assault rifle. "No more dead bodies."

She wasn't going to let him go on a killing spree. Something nagged at the back of her mind. Kane seemed as if he was out for vengeance. Who the hell had been nabbed that had so badly aroused Kane's anger? Sasha stepped in front of him. "We can capture these guys easily. I'll take the first one."

She waited tensely to see if he'd do it or not. She saw him push his gun behind his back. She breathed a sigh of relief.

"Agreed. Ready?"

"Ready," she said, every nerve ending tingling to life. She was good at what she'd been trained to do. In the old days, taking on three sentries would have been no sweat. But it wasn't the old days and she felt the need to be in top form.

The three men walked steadily toward her position. She felt Kane behind her. Knew he was readying himself for the coming fight as well. Though she knew he was a trained agent capable of taking care of himself, she didn't like to think of Kane in danger. She hoped he didn't kill any of these men. Sasha knew from her own walk on the dark side that the more you killed the harder it was to come back.

"Monitor the radio band and see if there's anyone else out there," she said to Orly.

"Gotcha, Nightshade. I'll report back as soon as I find something."

Kane dropped back into a fighting stance. "Go, Nightshade," he said.

She kicked her opponent as he moved past her position, knocking his weapon from his hand. He countered with a one-two jab toward her face. The blow connected with her cheekbone, stunning her. She pivoted into the punch and spun around to attack again, this time connecting with her opponent's ribs.

He moaned and stumbled backward. Sasha's breath ripped in and out. Damn, her face ached. She analyzed her position and, realizing that she had to put her body on autopilot, she ceased thinking about everything but surviving. This guy was twice her size and smelled as if he hadn't bathed in about a week. She wouldn't be able to call herself much of an agent if she couldn't bring him down.

Sasha diverted a blow as it came at her face. She *hated* getting hit in the head. As she spun away, he grabbed her hair, pulling her up short. Bringing both of her hands together, she reached behind her head for his wrist, applying a firm locking technique. Then, she twisted her body, and ducked under his arm. He tried to kick her but she lifted her leg and kneed him in the groin. He moaned as she twisted his arm behind his back and forced him to his knees.

Stopping beside him, she brought his hands together, using a zip cord to cuff him, then patted him down and found two guns and a knife on him. She took his weapons and put them in her pack.

Winning always brought its own kind of high. She'd forgotten how good it felt. She didn't examine it too closely but tucked the information away for later.

"Nightshade, you've got about two minutes before you're going to be outnumbered. Finish it and get out of there," Orly said in her ear.

"Gotcha," she replied.

She left the guy bound and headed toward Kane a few feet away. He was holding his own with the two assailants. Kane was one of the most skilled martial artists she'd ever met.

While she used a mix of tae kwon do and the street fighting her dad had taught her in hand-to-hand combat, Kane used an ancient art form and deadly skill.

But he was still just one man. She took a deep breath and a minute to analyze the fight, then jumped into the fray, at Kane's back. Feeling truly alive in the moment.

Fighting back to back with Kane. Each of them was equal in this moment.

She'd been bred for this and she realized as she fought with an energy that seemed to come from deep inside her that she'd denied this part of herself for too long. She couldn't live with the lies between her and Kane any longer.

"Let's finish this," she said to Kane.

"I'm trying," he said, connecting solidly with his opponent's sternum. Then used a judo chop to the neck.

The other guy attacked her with a strong kick that knocked her into Kane. He grunted and steadied her. "You okay?"

"Fine," she said.

She was aware of Kane and the third sentry fighting behind her and when she heard Kane groan, she wanted to go see if he was okay. But first things first.

She focused all her energy on the fight she was in. This guy had pulled his knife and took a swipe at her leg.

She kicked the weapon from his hand and out of reach. Knowing she had to make this attack count, she concentrated on hitting his neck and head. She struck him hard in the chest with a front kick, forcing his head into the wall. Jabbing his neck with her elbow, she grabbed one of his meaty wrists and brought it up behind his back, then forced his hands together and cuffed him.

She turned to help Kane but his opponent fell to the ground in a crumpled heap. Kane cuffed him.

"Two men are exiting the BMW and heading your way," Orly said. "Stop dicking around—get Kane and get out."

"Gotcha. Kane, we've got to get out of here. More men are headed this way."

Kane pulled his handgun and kept the assault rifle loosely at his side.

"You're just going to kill them," she said.

"No. I'm going to negotiate with them."

"Not tonight," Nightshade said. She closed the distance between them and embedded her thumb in his radial nerve. Kane tried to pull away but she pressed harder and his gun dropped to the ground as he lost all sensation in his arm.

"Sasha, no," he said.

"Sorry, lover, but I'm not letting you do this," she said. She shut out everything else, the sexy smell of Kane's cologne, the pain in her arms from pulling herself up the building, the dread of having to tell her husband she'd lied to him. And focused on the moment.

"Nightshade," he whispered again, twisting his head so their eyes met. In the shadows his were just dark pools of indigo.

For a moment it seemed her disguise fell away and that Kane was staring into her soul. Right down to the part she'd hidden from him for so long. She opened her mouth on a sigh.

"Going to let me go?" he asked, leaning close to her and letting his breath brush across her cheek.

He was flirting with her. God, it had been a long time since Kane had teased her. "Maybe."

"Maybe? I know how to change that to a yes." He leaned closer and ran his lips down the side of her neck, stopping at the base where her pulse was starting to beat a little faster.

She stepped back. For Kane's sake she couldn't let him do this. Couldn't let him stay free. Pulling a pair of handcuffs from her pocket, she quickly bound his wrists. Kane lashed out at her with his feet. Of course, he'd have to do it the hard way.

She stepped back into a defensive pose, realizing that the man she'd married had become a stranger to her.

Kane was no stranger to fighting—enemies and allies alike. But he wasn't himself tonight and neither was she. Although, a part of her was very much the outraged wife who'd been left in the country. Kane swung around, his graceful masculine body moving in perfect symmetry and kicking her feet out from under her.

Sasha wanted to take him down. They'd been driving toward this confrontation for a long time. She pushed herself to her feet and dropped back into a defensive pose. He circled around her. Sasha's nerves jangled. The aches and pains from her recent confrontation were starting to make themselves known and what she really wanted was to return to the Land Rover and get out the ice pack.

"Kane, you can't win."

"You're good, wife, I'll give you that. But I'm better."

That pissed her off. She quickly moved behind him and hit him squarely between the shoulder blades, knocking him to his knees. With his hands bound behind his back, his balance was hard to maintain. Stepping up behind him, Sasha straddled his neck with her thighs.

She tunneled her fingers into his thick black hair and pulled back, exposing his neck. "Who's better now?"

His breathing was uneven and he twisted his head as far as she allowed him. His breath was a hot brand against her inner thigh. He raked his teeth down the length of the pant fabric, causing rippling sensations along her skin.

Carefully she closed her thighs around his neck. He twisted his body, knocking her off balance. Sasha rolled to the ground, landing on her back. Before she could move, Kane fell on top of her, his head even with her breasts. He lifted his head and met her eyes. In an instant everything fell away except for Kane and this moment.

She'd missed this type of play between them. In the early days when they'd first started going out, Kane and she used to spar all the time like this.

"What went wrong?" he asked. "Where did the adventurous woman I first met go?"

She couldn't tell him. She didn't really know. She only knew that her last mission had changed something deep inside her and she'd never be the same again. She couldn't be.

She lifted her arms, pulled his head to hers and took the kiss she'd been wanting. A kiss that confirmed Kane was alive. A kiss that made the past melt away and the troubled future seem even colder than she'd realized it could be.

She'd missed his taste. All her barriers were down tonight and she'd forgotten how wonderfully seductive Kane could be when he put his mind to it. She didn't want to think about the reason he'd stopped seducing her. When she'd given him the cold shoulder, he hadn't taken it very well. She'd never been able to explain that it was either that or surrender her sanity.

She slipped her hand around his neck as her tongue entered his mouth. He moaned deep in his throat and she had a second's hesitation before she squeezed carefully on his carotid artery, rendering him unconscious. He fell limply on top of her and she brought her arms together around him to comfort him in a way he'd never allow when he was conscious.

Chapter 3

To the mind that is still the whole universe surrenders.

—Lao-tzu

Sasha carefully watched the men approach. She wished she knew what Kane was looking for. God, she ached from head to toe. She'd forgotten how to take a physical beating and shake it off. Or she was getting old. Because every hit she'd taken was screaming for an ice pack.

The man on the left walked with a slight limp and used a cane. He was thin and his head was shaved and he talked in a low voice to the man walking beside him. His voice didn't carry. She hoped Orly had got-

ten photos of both men. The second man was vaguely
familiar to her.

The one on the left wore a wool topcoat and his
companion wore a ratty old raincoat. She wasn't sure
if that information was relevant, but it seemed to her
that the men were underlings of Townsend's, not
peers. She itched to lift the assault rifle and just take
them both out with one quick bullet to the head. But
she wasn't an assassin, and killing a man who wasn't
threatening her went against the grain.

Dammit. She lowered the rifle. "Orly, Kane is
bound and unconscious, keep an eye on him. I need
Ano to send a detention crew for the three sentries
we captured and the body of the guard Kane took out.
I'm following the men to see if they'll lead me to
Townsend."

"Gotcha."

The men boarded one of the large shipping vessels down the dock. Sasha quickly bound Kane's feet
and left him hidden in the shadows.

"Run a trace on a ship called the *Eudora Man-
ning,*" she said. Then, using the international radio
code, she spelled it for him. Her mind was still on
Kane. Why was he doing this? He didn't like Townsend any more than she did. Townsend was at the top
of HMIA's most-wanted list. Every agent there still
felt Townsend's betrayal very strongly. But in the
last ten years he'd managed to continue evading
them. And Kane was acting exactly the same way
that had taken Townsend out of HMIA. Going out on
his own. Not following protocol.

"I'm going in for a closer look."

"Negative, Nightshade. Ano wants you to pull back."

Ano be damned. She was in the field and should be able to make her own decisions. "Orly, I'm close enough to get some good info. Request permission to board the *Eudora*."

"Relaying request."

Nightshade crouched in the shadows, waiting for permission to act. This was one reason why she'd left A.R.C. Despite their renegade status, there was still a chain of command that had to be followed. Nightshade started toward the ship, which was still anchored to the dock. The anchor was a large steel one that would be so easy to climb. She could be on the deck in a matter of minutes.

"Negative, Nightshade. Ano repeats orders to drop back."

"I'll finish a visual recon and then drop back."

"Relaying—"

"Don't relay, Orly." Did Ano not trust her to follow orders? Or did she not trust that Nightshade could complete the job? Neither question made Sasha feel any better about things.

"Gotcha."

Nightshade made a note of every detail she could, relaying information to Orly. The *Eudora* was a large ship probably used to transport animals of some kind. She noticed there were two lorries parked in the lower shipping bay. She didn't know if Townsend had his hostage somewhere in the bay or if these men that

Kane had been lying in wait for were just doing some recon themselves. Setting up the ship to move the hostage. But who was the hostage? It was time to get some answers from Kane.

She was reluctant to let the ship leave without finding out who the hostage was. She knew Kane well enough to guess that he felt some sort of responsibility for recovering them.

Yet, she had to play by the rules. This time there were others to think about. Others like Dylan who needed a mom, and Kane who was now a man she didn't really know.

Yet at the same time, he was that exciting, dangerous man she'd married. Sparring with him tonight had awakened every feminine instinct she had. Why now? Was it simply because they'd been apart so long? Or was it because she was once again experiencing that elixir she loved—the combination of danger, excitement and the one man who really made her feel alive.

"I'm returning to Kane. Should I take care of our captives?"

"Charity and Justice are on their way to apprehend them. We're to return to London for debriefing and interrogation."

"Gotcha."

Nightshade blended back into the shadows and walked swiftly to the spot where she'd left Kane. The night air was chilly yet invigorating. She stopped for a moment, closing her eyes and tipping her head backward. She was in the field again. Something she hadn't been sure she'd be able to manage until Dylan was in school.

But here she was. It was different than she'd expected it to be. She didn't feel as if it was real. Except for the aches and pains from the contact earlier with the sentries. She felt as though she was pretending to be someone else. When was she going to feel like herself again? When was the damn feeling of playacting going to go away?

Kane was conscious when she returned. His eyes were steely and she had the feeling that if she released his cuffs now he was going to have her in arm shackles in thirty seconds.

She knelt beside him, her gun in one hand, her eyes watchful. It would be foolhardy to try to retreat until they were sure that the two men were still on the ship.

"Orly, give me an exit route."

"Sit tight. There's some activity in the next berth. Will advise when you can move."

"Gotcha."

She turned to look at Kane. He watched her with a stare that was devoid of emotion. Inwardly she shivered. Her marriage wasn't going to survive this. And she wasn't sure she was too upset about it. Kane was more dangerous than facing a loaded gun because he made her react more strongly to things than she should. She would have left any other man out here.

"I couldn't let you do it," she said softly. She wasn't apologizing. But she wanted him to understand. Why did it matter? She'd carefully tucked away her emotions for Kane, channeling them into a more safer outlet—their son.

"Skip to the good part, Nightshade."

"*Is* there a good part?" she asked. Because she didn't see one. She saw her husband in jail for a long time and she and her son leaving Great Britain.

"Where are you taking me?" he asked, instead of answering.

"To Ano."

"And then you'll turn me over to Temple?"

She didn't say. He had to pay for his actions but he was her husband and she was torn. She didn't want to see him tried and found a traitor and then sent to jail.

He shifted to face her and in his eyes she saw something she hadn't seen there in a long time. He leaned up, so close that his lips brushed her cheek when he spoke. His breath smelled of mint and she wanted to taste him.

"There's still time, Nightshade. Set me free. I'll come back when I can."

God, she was tempted. She turned her head, brushing her lips against his stubble-covered jaw.

"No, Kane."

The two A.R.C. operatives arrived ten minutes after the *Eudora* left port. Orly was tracking the ship via satellite and was running photos of all the men captured or seen with Townsend through databases searching for names and connections.

For a minute Sasha wished she were back in Yorkshire in the safety of her country home, her little son sleeping down the hall and her husband still working in London but not on the outs. But she knew that some dreams weren't meant to be. And sometimes you had to realize the truth in that fact.

Sasha had escorted Kane to the command vehicle. He hadn't spoken to her since she'd refused to release him. And until she had a chance to really talk to him, she wasn't going to. She needed to understand his reasons. Plus, she was dealing with the aftermath of being close to once again breaking the rules and going after Townsend herself. She needed to cool down a little before she spoke to Ano.

She knew Ano wanted the information that Kane had, but Sasha knew she could've taken Townsend. Or at least disabled him enough to make him move slower.

Charity and Justice had arrived and were escorting the men she and Kane had captured into a white transit van with tinted windows similar to the ones used by MI-5. After the last man had been secured in the back and cuffed to the bench, Justice got behind the wheel and started radioing in the information that Sasha had gathered.

"Nice job, Nightshade. You'd never guess that you've been semiretired for almost two years," Charity said.

Charity was of Asian descent, the daughter of an American soldier and a Vietnamese woman. She'd been sent to America at the end of the U.S. occupation there and adopted by Ano. In some ways, Char-

ity was like her soul sister. They'd each been raised
by one parent and that parent was absolutely fanati-
cal about protection and global security. Rather than
wishing the world was a better place, their parents
were out there teaching them how to do it.

"It's not like I was sitting on my butt. I have been
doing a few jobs." Sasha realized she sounded defensive. She'd been raising her son, and that wasn't a
task to be ashamed of, but she'd been feeling lately
that it was. Part of the reason was her dad's attitude.
But a deeper part was her own longing and envy
every time she talked to Kane or another agent.

"Yeah, I heard about that exciting revamp of the
Yorkshire B and B's security system."

Nightshade heard the humor in Charity's voice.
"Very funny. I know it's not exciting, but it was important and I was able to stay with Dylan."

"How's he doing? Any more new teeth?"

"No new teeth. But he's started talking."

"Really? I can't wait to see him."

Sasha felt a tug in her heart. Charity was Dylan's
godmother and had been to visit only two weeks ago.
At that time Sasha had felt she had nothing in common with her friend. She'd felt as though they were
slipping apart as Charity talked in very vague terms
of her latest mission in South America. But now,
now she was back in the game.

And she'd have to thank Kane for it. Because she
realized that she wasn't really ready to let this part
of herself go. Protecting the security of tourists was
fine, but she'd forgotten what it was like to go head-

to-head with someone twice her size and come out the victor.

"You okay?" Charity asked.

Sasha realized she'd let the silence go too long. She also realized she wasn't doing as good a job of hiding her restlessness as she should. Though she and Charity were friends, she knew that the other woman would have no qualms about reporting to Ano that Sasha seemed unstable. "Yeah. Why wouldn't I be?"

Charity took her arm and pulled her a few feet away from the vehicles. "Kane."

"Ano called him Sterling. A wild card that had to be stopped at any cost."

"Mom can be a tough piece of business."

"I know. The hardest part was knowing she was right. Kane is…"

Charity watched her and Sasha found she couldn't say what she was thinking. That Kane had slipped past the control that all good agents had. It was the only thing that stopped an agent from crossing over to the dark side. The only thing that made you keep working for a system with faults and foibles. A system that was inherently fallible because it was made up of humans who made mistakes. Who were tempted and easily lead astray at times.

Charity reached out and gave Sasha a quick hug. "I'm here if you need me."

"Thanks. I'll handle this."

"You always do."

"You going to chat all night or can we get back to work?" Justice called.

Charity gave her partner the finger, then turned and walked away from Sasha. Sasha watched her go then headed toward the Land Rover where Orly and Kane waited for her. She needed every shield she had in place. She wasn't taking Kane to Ano until she had some answers, and knowing Kane, it wasn't going to be easy to get them.

Sasha paused outside the vehicle then realized that she was acting like a wimp. Not a wimp. *Just a woman.* One who wasn't ready to have another fight with her husband.

Kane had brought endless complications to her life. All of the unrest stemmed from his presence. Even her last mission, which had gone horribly wrong, was tied to him. She'd been distracted by the new man in her life.

She'd been weaker than she normally was because her life had been so full in those first few months of their becoming lovers, and Sasha had forgotten the truth she'd always known. That life didn't work out for the best just because you wanted it to.

She reached up and opened the back door. Kane was bound similarly to the men he'd helped her apprehend. The image made her heart squeeze in her chest. She could see how uncomplicated her life in Leeds really was. And how her soul craved that solitude.

Her soul also craved adventure, but not like this. She climbed into the command vehicle. A thin piece of tinted bulletproof glass separated her and Kane from Orly. Orly had the vehicle in motion as soon as Sasha shut the door.

She sat down next to Kane in the back seat. He wouldn't look at her and she felt an explosion deep in her soul. And part of that explosion was guilt. Rationally she knew she'd had no other choice. Kane couldn't risk his life and the lives of other operatives to appease a villain like Townsend.

If he hadn't gone crazy none of this would have happened.

"Did you give Orly the microchip?" she asked after a few minutes had passed. All of the data from the STAR list had been coded onto a computer chip. Easy to transport, easy to hide.

He didn't say anything.

Nice. She thought. She didn't want to have to rough up Kane to get information from him. And he knew it. He knew she couldn't do it. But there were other avenues at her disposal. Avenues she'd never use with any other man but she could with Kane.

She leaned closer to him, pressing against his side. She rubbed her hand down his chest and felt his breath quicken. Her own senses stirred to life. It had been too long since she and Kane had made love. She refused to let this be anything other than a simple seduction to get information.

"Sasha, don't," he said.

Finally he looked at her, and what she saw in his shuttered gaze made her heart beat faster. He wasn't immune to her, but then sexual compatibility had never been their problem. It was the emotional stuff that always caught her unaware. And it did tonight as well. Everything she'd felt for Kane converged, the lust, the anger, the hurt, the disappointment, swirling inside her head and making it impossible to divorce herself fully from the situation.

Just be an agent. But she couldn't be—especially when she was so close to him that she could feel his warmth and feel the brush of each exhalation against her shoulder. She shifted farther away from him, lifting one hand to brush back her hair but encountering the black leather of her mask.

"You've left me no choice."

"Really?" he asked in that silky voice of his that never failed to make her respond.

She'd started a game she had little chance of winning. "Really."

"And we all know you'll do anything for the Company."

If only that was why she was here. Did Kane really think the only reason she'd come after him was because of her job? How little he knew her. She wryly acknowledged to herself that she'd never really let him know her. But it hurt all the same that he hadn't tried. "I'm not doing this for the Company."

"Then who?" he asked, arching one eyebrow.

She said nothing. This was her interrogation not his. She was the one asking the questions. She wanted to know what was going on. Who was the hostage? Where was the hostage being held? Why had Kane taken the STAR list and did he still have it?

But he persisted. "Me?"

Suddenly it was too much. "Don't say it like that. You know I'd do anything to save you."

"Do I? Then why am I living in London while you stay in Leeds?"

"You're the one who moved out." And she'd never really understood why he left. She'd put distance between them after Dylan was born. But only when she'd realized how intense the love she felt for her son was. She couldn't stem those feelings, and having more than one person to care for made her weak—vulnerable. Something she could never really afford to be. She still had powerful enemies out there looking for her.

Of course, she hadn't really done a good job of not caring about Kane, witnessed by tonight's events. And the man didn't even realize it.

"Yes, I did," he said quietly.

She didn't want to have this discussion. Not now. Maybe not ever. "Just tell me where the information Ano wants is."

He tipped his head back against the window and closed his eyes. "I don't have it."

"Dammit, Kane. HMIA says you do."

"I meant on me."

"Where is it?" she asked. She wasn't going to play games with him. Very few of her adversaries had ever made her want to lose her cool the way Kane did.

"Going to rough me up?" he challenged, waggling his eyebrows at her. He was a charming man most of the time. She was tempted to kick Orly out of the van and drive away. Go get Dylan and just disappear with Kane. But that was only a dream.

"Do I really have to?" she asked. Maybe she

should have taken herself off the mission. Maybe she wasn't the woman she'd always believed herself to be.

"What if I said yes?"

She knew he was toying with her. That he wanted her to have doubts and he was definitely playing on them. She refused to let him do it. "Don't. Do you think this is easy for me?"

He cursed savagely under his breath.

"Sasha…"

He drew her name out. Speaking to her in that silky, deep voice of his that painted sensual shivers all over her nerve endings. She pulled her black leather mask off and tossed it onto the opposite bench.

"Why are you going after Townsend on your own?" she asked at last. If he confided in her, they'd be able to work together to make this more than a rogue agent betraying his government.

"It's my assignment."

"It *was* your assignment. What went wrong? Explain it to me, Kane. Make me understand what's going on."

"I got tired of never being able to act. So I took matters into my own hands."

"Convince me to help you," she said softly. If he said the right words, she'd abandon the Company and join him in his quest for justice.

He turned his head and stared at her with those glacial gray eyes of his. "I don't think so."

Chapter 4

Knowledge comes, but wisdom lingers.
            —Alfred, Lord Tennyson

Orly drove effortlessly through the early-morning traffic on the M3. Sasha stared out the window watching the sun breaking. Realizing with a touch of irony that this was the first sunrise she and Kane had seen together in a really long time.

They were entering the city limits of Winchester. She pretended to be interested in the scenery. But signs for Bird World, Lego Land, Ascot and Windsor didn't hold her interest. Only a dark-haired, brooding man who she'd once known intimately but who was now watching her with a guarded look.

"Where are we going?" he asked.

"To London." He sounded tired but didn't look it. She knew him well enough to be aware that he was gathering himself for the coming battle. And there was no way he was going to allow her or any one else to take him into custody. Again she wondered why he was determined to remain outside the Agency.

"That's not where Townsend is," Kane said quietly.

Sasha knew that if she were the one in cuffs she'd be yelling at Kane, raging to make him let her go. But Kane just got calmer as they put distance between themselves and Southampton. "Do you know where he is?"

"My source said Southampton."

"We were all over that city today, Kane. Townsend wasn't there."

"Maybe not, but his second in command, Renault, was. I could have gotten Townsend's location from the man."

"How? By beating it out of him?"

He shrugged but didn't answer.

"What's gotten into you, Kane? Give this up."

"Never."

The conviction in his voice startled her. Kane didn't persist when a cause was lost. He'd always been very rational. "Why? We're not on a short clock now. Tell me everything."

Kane stared straight at her and for a split second she thought he'd tell her but then he blinked. "It's too dangerous. I can't tell you."

This wasn't about doing the job. Kane knew she

could. So what did he think he was protecting her against? "I think I'm able to defend myself."

"Not against everything."

Truer words had never been spoken. But Kane had never seen her fail and she wondered if he sensed her own self-doubt, if he had caught glimpses of her own confusion with life and with herself that had to have leaked out. "I've tangled with Townsend before."

"Sasha, why can't you ever just trust me?" he asked, frustration in his voice.

She shrugged. What could she say to him? "Is that why you left?"

"No. Trust is only part of it."

She didn't want to tell him that something had changed inside her. That freeing and seeing her dark side had made her realize that she didn't know herself and she barely trusted that other part. "Trust is a two-way street."

"Yeah, it is. Untie me and I'll tell you everything."

She knew this moment was going to come. And honestly, she wanted to free Kane. If he was free, they would be equals again and maybe he'd tell her what the hell was going on. "If you try to escape…"

"You'll shoot me in the back, I know."

"No, Kane. But I will recapture you and I'll be pissed."

He cocked his head to the side. "Good."

"You like it when I'm mad."

"It's the only time when you aren't holding Dylan that I see any real emotion on your face."

"Am I cold?"

"You weren't always."

"What was our big mistake?"

"You tell me."

"I...I don't know."

The British countryside flashed by and Sasha turned away from her husband, from a man whom she'd once thought she knew but who had depths to him, she now realized, that she'd never really explored. She pulled the key to the cuffs from her pocket and freed Kane. The first thing he did was extend his long legs then reach over his head to stretch his arms.

Suddenly it seemed as if she were in a cage with a lion. She felt the restlessness in him and knew if the Land Rover were a little larger he'd be prowling from one end to the other. She watched him, every instinct on hyperalert. Ready to follow him if he opened the door and jumped.

God, she really hoped he didn't do that because she still ached from the earlier tussle. She was a little out of shape and hitting the ground and rolling wasn't going to make her feel any better.

The silence grew between them and she realized he was watching her. Eyeing her, actually, probably trying to ascertain the best way to disarm her.

"Tell me what's going on."

"Townsend has taken Anna."

"Your sister Anna?"

Kane nodded.

"Why?"

"I don't know. Temple and I were working on infiltrating a drug-smuggling ring. I didn't think we'd come anywhere near Townsend."

Bruce Temple had a large family with four sisters. Kane and Temple were brothers in all but blood. Another piece of the puzzle fell into place for Sasha. She'd wondered why Temple wasn't with Kane; he didn't want to endanger anyone else.

"Are you sure he has Anna?"

Kane reached into his back pocket and pulled out a Polaroid picture. Sasha took it from him, glancing down and seeing something that made blood rush in her ears. Her fourteen-year-old sister-in-law bound and gagged, with a copy of the *Mirror* newspaper with yesterday's date.

For the second time in her life, Sasha felt betrayed not only by her own instincts but by her boss. She tried to think rationally but couldn't. Her gut urged her to pound on the window and tell Orly to turn them the hell around. They needed to get back on the trail of Townsend. And not be following him via a very sophisticated tracking system, but actually be on his ass so that he didn't make land with Anna.

Anna, the sweet fourteen-year-old who thought that the world was her oyster. Just last week, Sasha had spoken to her. They'd made plans for a shopping trip and...oh, God, Sasha closed her eyes. She wasn't prepared for this. She realized that she hadn't done a very good job of protecting herself from the emotions she'd sought to hide from.

First, Kane brought her away from the relative

security of Leeds, and back into the action that she'd promised herself she'd stay away from until Dylan was old enough to understand. And now, Anna reminded her of the mistakes she'd made when her own sister, Caroline, was kidnapped.

"I won't rest until everyone associated with her kidnapping is dead." Kane's voice promised the kind of retribution that Sasha associated with outlaws. He'd crossed the line between government official and vigilante and she wasn't sure she could talk him into coming back across the line.

Sasha glanced at Kane. In his eyes was the kind of hell that she'd let consume her once before. She turned away from Kane, knowing she had to act. First, she had to secure the information he'd taken. She was beginning to believe that Kane wouldn't actually use the information, but she wasn't willing to bet all those lives on it.

Sasha pushed the intercom button and ordered Orly to stop. He pulled to the side of the road, and thirty seconds later joined them in the back of the Rover.

Orly's gaze scanned the interior, noted Kane's freedom, but he didn't comment. That was one of the things she liked about Orly.

"I need to make some calls. Watch Kane," Sasha said.

"This vehicle is the most secure place to make them. Can it wait five minutes?" Orly asked. He ran his hands through his spiked hair. His eyes were full of questions, which he kept to himself.

"Why?" she asked. Orly might be her partner but she'd never really understood how his mind worked.

She knew he saw things that she didn't and she trusted him in that area.

"I can find a place to grab some food at the next exit," he said.

She nodded. Orly went back up front and they were moving again.

"What are you going to do?" Kane asked.

Sasha glanced over at him. She should send him up front with Orly and call the sergeant major right now. But she put it off. She'd been betrayed before and she didn't like it. "Verify some facts."

"Sasha, I might not be husband of the year but I wouldn't lie about this." The sincerity in his voice cut her deeply, making her realize how deep a gap existed between the two of them. A gap that she wasn't sure she'd ever be able to bridge. She hugged herself, rubbing her hands over her arms in an attempt to find some warmth in the cold morning.

"I know. But did Dad?"

Kane stretched his arm out and pulled her against his side. She resisted him and heard his aggrieved sigh. Then she tentatively rested her body against him. She hated that feminine weakness inside her.

It was the part of herself she trusted the least and the part that Kane inevitably called to the surface. She'd craved a distance between them.

Kane said nothing, only stroked his hand down her arm. She felt the tension in him and knew that he wasn't going to be content to allow her to gather information for too long before he made his move. She hoped to hell she was ready to make a decision, because she knew Kane wasn't going to come peacefully.

"I'm sure your dad had his reasons for his actions."

Sasha slid away from Kane. Her father and Kane had some strange sort of bond that Sasha didn't really understand. Kane had tried to explain it to her one time, saying only that they both had a vested interest in keeping her happy, but she'd never really understood.

"Me too. But were they his own or Ano's? Ano knows Dad well enough to use him to get to me."

"Why would she do that?"

"I don't know. Unless she thought that I'd join you and we'd rescue Anna together. I'm just not sure of anything."

"I'm sure, Sasha. I'll allow you to make your calls but I'm not going in meekly."

"What are you going to do?"

He raised both eyebrows. "Come with me and I'll tell you everything."

She didn't want to think about that now. First, she had to figure out who knew that Anna had been taken. Because there was no way that HMIA wouldn't have mentioned that fact. If her father had lied to her, Sasha wasn't sure what she'd do. Send Orly back to get Dylan because she couldn't trust her dad with her son.

If it had been Ano, then that meant that once again she was going to be outside of the Agency. Because she knew exactly how Kane felt. Anna had become her little sister when they married and she wasn't going to risk losing another sister. Not again.

"Do you have a plan?"

"Of course I do."

She'd learned from her mistakes. She wouldn't let rage consume her and she'd keep Kane in line. Orly pulled off the motorway and found a small restaurant that was serving breakfast.

"Kane, don't do anything rash."

He made no promises to her but gave her a grin that reminded her why she'd fallen in love with him four years ago. Only, this morning she saw a dangerous kind of revenge lurking in his eyes and she wasn't sure if he'd invited her along to keep her out of his way or if he'd invited her because he needed another gun.

The sergeant major answered his phone on the first ring. His voice was gruff and Sasha knew that her number was scrambled and he didn't know who he was speaking to.

"It's me, Dad."

"Did you get Kane?" he asked.

She didn't answer him. She wasn't sure she wanted to give him any information that he might pass on to Ano. She'd put her dad in an awkward position when she'd gone after Caroline's killers and turned her back on A.R.C. before. She didn't want to do it again. "I have to ask you a few questions."

He sighed. She could imagine him sitting in the solarium at the back of the house. Dylan would be up and playing at this hour.

"Dylan's fine. He's been up for about forty-five minutes. I fed him that dried cereal and we talked

about how a man should be doing his own business
and not waiting on someone else to change him."

Sasha smiled to herself. Her unease at questioning her father abated for a minute at the image of her
dad as a grandfather. "Thanks for the rundown. Give
him a hug for me."

"You okay, girl?"

"Yeah," she said. She forced her thoughts off her
son and back on to the task at hand. It was almost
seven in the morning and if they were going to act...
hell, a part of her already knew she was going to act.
"I need to ask you about the mission you sent me on."

"What about it?" he asked in that machine-gun
manner that he'd honed on young privates and other
subordinates over the years. It was the same tone
he'd used to keep her in line all those years ago.

"Did you know that Anna was the hostage?" Sasha
asked point-blank. Tired of trying to guess if the one
person she'd always counted on had betrayed her.

"Anna Sterling?" he asked. The shock in his voice
could have been acting but she doubted it. Her father
wasn't much on subterfuge.

"Yes."

"Jesus. No wonder Ano said we were on a tight
clock," he said. Then she heard him curse more
strongly under his breath.

"Is that a no?" she asked, unwilling to take any leaps
in logic. She wanted everything clearly documented.

"Do you honestly believe I'd keep that info to myself?" he asked in that quiet voice of his that let her
know she'd disappointed him.

At one time, no he wouldn't have. He would have given her every detail and made sure she understood the costs. But losing Caroline had changed everything and now her dad didn't really know how she'd react. Part of her wondered if he'd kept that information a secret because he was afraid she'd compromise the mission. "Nothing is what it seemed. I'm not sure what to believe."

He snorted. "Nice, kid. You don't even trust your old man."

"My old man has lied to me in the past," she reminded him. Twice. The first time she'd been six and had come home from school upset because she was the only kid who didn't have a mom. And he'd told her that her mother had died giving birth to her, which she'd found out was a lie fourteen years later when an eighteen-year-old Caroline had shown up on their doorstep. Having a younger sister meant their mother had been alive for at least part of Sasha's life.

The sergeant major had explained that he and Tessa, Sasha and Caroline's mother, couldn't live together, so they'd each taken a kid to raise.

The second time he'd lied was when he'd told her she'd done the right thing in saving Seth, Caroline's son, and leaving Caroline behind to defend herself. Sasha shook herself and forced her thoughts back to the present.

"Only to protect you, kid."

She didn't like the way he said that. She protected herself. She'd learned that lesson at a high cost and would never forget it. "I know. That's why I had to ask."

"Well, this time I was in the dark. I wouldn't have let you walk into that situation. Did you get Kane?" he asked.

Sasha saw no point in keeping it from her dad. Charity would be in London in about forty-five minutes and Ano would know everything. By that time she and Kane would be on the trail, after Anna. "Yeah, I got him."

"Is Kane still with you?" he asked. Her dad knew Kane as well as she did. The fact that Kane was still here told her that on some level he still trusted her.

"Yes, but I'm not taking him to Ano."

Her dad said nothing for a few minutes; she knew he was running different scenarios through his mind and analyzing the outcome. She thought she heard Dylan in the background and she longed to pick him up and hold him. To keep him safe in her arms.

Because if Townsend went after Anna, what was to stop him from going after Kane's son? And that image had the power to paralyze Sasha.

"Think good and hard about this, kid. She won't take you back again."

"I know that."

"Stay in touch, Sasha. I'm here if you need me."

"You trained me to take care of myself."

"Hell, that doesn't mean you can't ask for help."

"Doesn't it?"

"What do you need from me?"

"Nothing, Dad."

"I'm serious, Sasha. I'm on your side, girl."

She took a deep breath. Did she need her father's

help? He could slow down Ano and give her and Kane a lead, but that would mean involving him in the mission and she wanted Dylan far removed it.

"I can't risk it," she said at last.

"I won't let anything happen here."

"I know that. You raised me, didn't you."

"That's right I did. Make me proud, kid."

"I'll try."

She rang off before he could say anything else, knowing that come hell or high water, she'd made her decision and she'd see it to the end.

Chapter 5

We carry within us the wonders we seek without.
                                        —Sir Thomas Browne

Sasha sat in the Rover by herself, thoughts circling through her head. Contact Ano or just go. If she left without contacting her boss, she knew that they'd have a slight lead. But for Anna's sake, she wanted to have every resource at her fingertips and A.R.C. was a powerful resource.

"Dammit." She wasn't sure what kind of game Ano was playing. But Sasha had learned a long time ago that working on her own, relying only on herself, had left her feeling…well, just feeling too damn vulnerable, and she wasn't about to get on that merry-go-round again.

She lifted the handset just as the back door opened and Kane and Orly climbed into the vehicle. A cool morning wind filled the vehicle and Sasha shivered. Kane took a seat near the rear and passed her a cup of coffee.

"Thanks," she said quietly.

Kane had gathered himself together in the time he'd been gone. There was a determination and a force of will in him that he always kept carefully hidden behind a jovial exterior. But that charming man wasn't in residence today. Today, Kane was a rough-and-ready warrior ready to go after his sister and make anyone who dared touch his family pay.

"Well?" Kane asked.

Sasha didn't know. Choosing between Kane and the Company. She knew Ano would demand Sasha turn Kane over to her. And she knew that without Kane turning over the information he'd taken, Ano wouldn't allow him to leave.

"Tell me your plan," she said at last.

Kane rubbed his eyes and then took a sip of his coffee. "Find out where Townsend is and then force him to tell me where Anna is. If I have to use the STAR list I will."

"That's it? What have you got, a death wish?" Orly asked.

Kane shrugged. Sasha's mind swirled. As far as plans went, that wasn't a great one. But it wasn't exactly a bad one either. "What about backup?"

"I couldn't ask Temple to go on this mission because he's got family."

She couldn't believe what she was hearing. Didn't he realize that he was the center of Dylan's little world and that she depended on him as well? "You've got family too, Kane."

He gave her one of those looks of his that cut right through every protective barrier she had and made her feel as if her soul was laid bare to him. "It hasn't felt like it lately."

And that was the heart of the matter, as far as they both were concerned. They didn't feel like a family anymore. Sasha turned away from her husband and his cold gray eyes. Decision time. In her mind her father whispered for her to suck it up and just make a decision.

Orly was staring at the computer screen pretending not to hear, and she appreciated his discretion. "You followed your sources to Southampton, but do you know where Townsend is?"

"My intel says that Townsend has been using a port in France to switch from sea to land," Kane said. He'd moved as well, leaning around her to study the same screen. She felt the tension in him and knew that he needed to act soon, or he'd go crazy. "But my gut says he hasn't left England yet."

"Where is he transporting to?" Sasha asked, her husky voice too low for her own comfort.

"Izmir," Kane said.

"Turkey?"

Kane nodded.

"Where was Anna taken?"

"I'm not sure. I didn't even investigate from that end."

"Just went off half-cocked with a gun in each hand and vengeance burning in your eyes."

"I'm a man of action."

"You're a crazy man. Orly, see if you can pull up an incident report about Anna's abduction. Then we'll go back to the scene of the kidnapping and start there."

Orly put on his headphones and went to work. Kane slid down the bench. Sasha looked over at him. Knowing that there was a wide gulf between them. Realizing that she was responsible for it. And understanding that she didn't know how to make it go away.

"I'll help you but you have to turn the list over to me."

"I can't. Townsend knows that the Agency won't give it to him. He's going to kill her."

Did he want to die? She wanted to ask him but couldn't with Orly sitting right next to them. What was going on with her husband? Because it seemed as if he'd been taking these risks with his life before Anna had been taken.

"Okay. We have to contact Ano. I know you think you can take Townsend but I want some backup."

"Do what you must."

She took that to mean he'd be leaving them soon. "They have resources that a man on the outside can't touch."

"Those resources aren't available to me, Sasha. You know it. I made my decision and I'm not going back."

"Why?"

"They wanted to wait. To let hostage negotiators have a try at changing his mind."

"Townsend doesn't do that."

"Exactly. So my superiors said they'd do everything in their power but their hands were tied. Mine weren't."

"Kane, rage is its own kind of shackle."

"I don't give a damn," he said and turned away.

Sasha went back to Orly. "You're going to love me, boss lady," he said. "Anna was taken in Leicester Square. She was with three of her friends, Hannah Smythe, Tamara Jones and Lisa Pennington. They all gave statements to the police that boiled down to the fact that a black BMW with tinted windows pulled up to the curb, a man got out and called Anna's name. She turned toward him and two men grabbed her from behind, pushing her into the car. Which then sped away."

Clearly, Orly was glad to be back in the thick of things, but she also sensed a certain anger inside him. He'd met Anna Sterling as well. She wasn't sure this was the right place for them. Or the right mission, and that worried her. "Let's go back to London and see what we can find."

Jane Sterling seemed to have aged ten years since Anna had been taken. She was an elegantly coiffed woman with honey-blond hair and bright green eyes. Her house was located in Esher, a very upscale neighborhood. The floors were all hardwood and the furniture antiques. The first time Sasha had dinner there she'd been so nervous she'd broken one of the Waterford crystal goblets.

The butler showed them into the formal living room. Kane paced around it. He was haggard and clearly tired. But from her own experiences with losing her sister, she knew that sleeping was almost impossible. Every time you closed your eyes you were forced to deal with another image.

Though Sasha normally wasn't much of a hugger, she went straight to her mother-in-law and wrapped her arms around her.

Jane shuddered and hugged her back. "We'll get Anna back for you," Sasha promised.

"Kane's been great about making Anna a number-one priority."

That was the understatement of the year. Sasha figured that Kane wouldn't tell his mom that he'd had to actually leave the Agency in order to try to rescue Anna the way he wanted to.

"That's my job, Mum. We have a few questions for you."

"I've already told the police everything I know."

"Sasha's new to the case and just hearing you re-tell it might help."

"Very well."

She sat down on one of the wingback chairs. Sasha sat down across from her and took a small notepad from her bag. Orly was outside in the Rover making arrangements for them to interview the girls who'd been shopping with Anna.

"Would you like something to eat or drink?" Jane asked.

"No thanks," Sasha said.

"No," Kane added.

"How well did Anna know the girls she was shopping with?"

"Fairly well. They all attend Charterhouse together. Every Saturday they go to Leicester Square for a movie and then stay to hang out with their friends."

"When did they start doing this?" Sasha asked.

"Three months ago when Hannah joined them at school. Prior to that, they'd hang out at school."

"We're going to question the girls. When were you notified that Anna was taken?"

"Almost immediately. Tamara called her mother, Laura, who in turn called me. I called the police and Kane."

"Mother and I made arrangements to meet at Leicester Square. I talked to the girls after the police were done with them."

"This kidnapping makes no sense," Jane said. "We have nothing of value to be bargained for."

But she *did* have something very valuable in her son. Kane must have been thinking along the same lines. He turned toward the window and she saw him bow his head. Guilt was a curious thing, she realized. She felt guilty for pushing Kane away from her. He felt guilty that his career had made him a target. And Jane felt guilty about something…what, Sasha didn't know.

"Try not to worry. Is there anything else you can remember? When you got to the scene, did you talk to anyone?"

"I'm afraid I wasn't much help," Jane said. She closed her eyes. "I can't believe my baby is missing."

"She won't be for long, Mum. I promise you, I'll get her back."

"We won't rest until she's home."

"My father is watching Dylan at our place. Do you want to join him there?"

"No. Thank you, but Lydia is on her way here now."

Lydia was Kane's middle sister and worked in Milan for an Italian fashion house. Sasha stood. She didn't have any more questions. Her heart wept for Jane and it didn't take much of an imagination to realize how she'd feel if Dylan were missing.

The fact that she had the same dangerous profession as Kane made her want to return home, take her son and hide away. To hell with rescuing the world, she wanted to protect her son. But another part of her realized that life couldn't really be lived by hiding in shadows and that's all she'd be doing.

"If you think of anything, call us." Sasha stood up and shifted her purse on her shoulder.

"I will," Jane said.

Kane came over to his mom and she hugged him tight. "You be careful. I have enough to worry about with Anna missing."

"I will be."

Nearly two hours later they were in Leicester Square. The arcades were filled with kids and lots of noise. Sasha had contacted Ano and advised her of the situation. Charity was interrogating the men they'd captured. But so far nothing new had been learned.

"I need the details once Charity gets them," Sasha said. There was a hell of a lot of ground to cover. And every second that they delayed increased the tension in Kane and the likelihood of them not getting to Anna in time.

"Negative, Nightshade. Bring Sterling to me."

Sasha wasn't about to do that. She'd already made her decision, which was why she was here conducting her own investigation. Kane prowled along beside her like a caged tiger and Sasha had the very real feeling that before too long he was going to snap and she was going to have to cuff him again.

But not right now. Sasha sank back into the leather seat in the com room on the Land Rover.

"I'm not going to do it, Ano. Give me some time. I'll get the STAR list back from him. He's not going to surrender it without a fight. I think I can convince him to trust me," Sasha said, hoping she wouldn't have to say more.

But inside, her anger was building slowly. She was mad at Kane for doing something incredibly stupid and for not calling her first. She was mad at Ano for sending her after her husband. She was pissed at Townsend for once again striking out at her and coming too close to her family.

She wondered if he knew about her connection to Kane. She doubted it. After all, her Nightshade persona was excellent cover and Orly had found no signs that anyone had been digging for information on her.

"I know."

Confirmation of her suspicions didn't make her

feel better. Ano had her own agenda and Sasha was very aware of how hard it was to keep A.R.C.'s reputation within the changing intelligence community. Recovering that microchip would give Ano a nice coup, especially with Interpol, HMIA and other organizations all searching for it. "I suspected as much. I don't want to do this on my own. I need your resources and some backup."

Sasha heard the clicking of keys and pictured Ano in that office of hers. She was one of the most intelligent women Sasha had ever met and was capable of doing more than one thing at the same time. Not mindless tasks, either.

"Sterling is an outlaw. We don't know which way he'll turn. I'll give you thirty-six hours and then I'm taking you out of the game."

"Okay." Sasha's gut tightened. This time she needed to do it by the book or risk slipping over to the darker side of her personality. The one side she didn't really want to face again. But she wasn't going to beg. She wasn't going to reveal that weakness to anyone. She could keep it together and get Anna back.

"He's not an outlaw. He's an enraged relative." What was the difference? Sasha knew where Kane was and she knew before too much longer she was going to have to confront her own demons and maybe convince him to give up on his own quest for vengeance.

"Exactly, enraged. He's not the man he once was." Ano's words echoed the fear in her heart.

And he never would be again. Nightshade knew that and it scared her. She didn't want Kane to be lost in the same wasteland she was. She needed him to be the man he'd always been. And part of her was afraid that maybe she didn't know that man.

"Sasha…"

There was something in Ano's voice that reminded her of when she was a child. Ano had always been a wise woman who had answers to every question that Sasha had. Even the ones she didn't want answered. Ano was always unflinchingly honest, and today, Sasha didn't want to hear what Ano had to say. "Yes."

"Bring him here. Together we'll find the information and return it to HMIA. Then we can concentrate on retrieving the hostage."

"I can't, Ano. I've lost one sister and I'm not going to lose another."

Silence buzzed on the open line and Sasha was very aware that she'd revealed something that she shouldn't have. But Ano had to have known that Caroline was behind her involvement. Ano had probably counted on that when she'd dispatched the sergeant major to rouse her from the country.

"Saving this girl won't bring Carolina back."

Nightshade pretended she didn't hear Ano's words. The keys stopped clicking. She closed her eyes and for a minute she saw Carolina and Anna together. Saw both sisters, the one she'd left behind and the one who was in danger. And for a minute she felt the black rage that she'd used to find some peace for Carolina. Nightshade knew then that she was going to have to follow that path again.

"Just get the microchip with the database on it and I'll give you backup."

"I'll try."

"Don't cross me on this, Nightshade. That chip is worth more than the girl's life."

"Not to my way of thinking." Nightshade hung up the phone and exited the Land Rover.

She'd learned more about herself while she'd been in Leeds than she'd suspected. Because before she would have never contemplated what she was contemplating now. She wanted the chip, Anna Sterling and Townsend.

And she wasn't going to settle for anything less than the three of them where they belonged. Anna at home with her family. The chip safely away where it couldn't harm any more agents' lives or families. And Townsend serving life in a maximum-security cell.

Chapter 6

No one outside ourselves can rule us inwardly.

—The Buddha

Sasha had changed into jeans, a sweater and her leather jacket earlier. She'd left Kane with Orly questioning a group of boys who had seen the men who took Anna. Now, as she walked across the street, she felt as if someone was watching her. Without altering her stride she ducked down a narrow alleyway and then ran to the end to crouch behind a Dumpster.

The morning was cloudy and cold. Sasha unzipped the jacket and reached behind her to grasp the gun in the holster at the small of her back. She pulled out the Glock and waited. Had Ano sent one of her assassins after Nightshade and Sterling? She'd have to warn Orly about the risks of staying with them on this mission.

Every nerve was on hyperalert as she remained crouched down. While a part of her rational mind said the follower was nothing more than a man following a pretty woman across the street, her gut said there was a trained professional on her trail. When the stranger slowed and then eased his way into the alley, she knew her gut had been correct.

She closed out everything around her. The chill of the air still penetrated her clothing but she no longer felt it. The noises of the street still filled the air but she no longer heard it. The shift of gravel under the man's shoes was a minute sound, but she absorbed and calculated the weight and height of the person who'd made that step. She focused on the target and brought her gun up, preparing to fire. That image disturbed the mother in her. And Sasha understood that she couldn't be both women at the same time. She had to choose, and to stay alive the choice had to be, for right now, to be an agent.

But the blond-haired man wasn't a stranger. When Sasha glanced around the Dumpster and met his gray-green gaze, she clicked on the safety and stood up. *This* was unexpected. She could have killed an assassin or one of Townsend's goons.

But not a man she'd had to dinner. A man who'd stood up with her and Kane at their wedding. A man who was her son's godfather. "Temple."

Bruce was clearly tired. And his face was lined

with more than fatigue. He cautiously surveyed the area behind her and Sasha knew he was looking for Kane.

"Sterling. Though not the one I'm searching for."

Sasha had no idea what to say. She didn't think that Temple knew her identity as Nightshade, but he had to have guessed that she was here with Kane. She also knew that she couldn't let him find her husband. And she didn't have what he was searching for. That damn microchip.

"How'd you find us?" Sasha asked.

Temple stared at her for so long she was afraid he wasn't going to answer. He had no reason to trust her. She'd just pulled a gun on him. "I know Kane as well as I know myself," Temple explained. "It was simply a matter of knowing how he thinks."

"Even now?" Sasha asked. He had to have followed them to Leicester Square, because Kane had been hell-bent on beating information out of Townsend's men. Not starting an investigation.

Temple gave her a half smile that wasn't as friendly as she was sure he'd hoped it would be. There were too many teeth in that expression. "Even now."

"What are you going to do?" she asked. Maybe Temple could be convinced to join them. They needed another gun at their backs. Townsend wasn't going to be easy to find and the more people they had looking, the better the chances that they could recover Anna—alive.

Temple knew the stakes. And Townsend had to be at the top of Temple's most-wanted list simply because he'd shaken up the only home Temple had ever had—the brother-like bond between him and Kane.

But the glacial look in Temple's eyes told Sasha that Bruce wasn't here to offer his services. He had his own agenda and his own enemy—Kane.

"Get that microchip and bring him in."

Sasha didn't like the way he said that. The sooner they found Anna the better for all concerned. "Dead or alive?"

"Dead—no. Beaten to a bloody pulp—hell, yes."

Temple had a look in his eyes that said he was good and angry and nothing was going to stop him. Sasha sighed deep inside herself. This was what happened when personal and professional lines were crossed. She had to get that chip from Kane. Temple was only one agent. She was sure that other intelligence organizations would start sending operatives to retrieve the chip as well.

"I can't let you do that."

"Sasha, I know he's your husband, but you're no match for a trained agent."

"I'm not your average stay-at-home mom, Temple."

"No, you aren't." Temple agreed. "Where is he?"

"If I promised to return the chip, would you let it go?" she asked, wildly wondering how she could possibly promise such a thing.

"No."

"Why not?"

"He betrayed me, Sasha. Surely you don't condone that."

"You know Townsend has Anna?"

"Yes. I ache for her but that doesn't mean I can forget my duty. That has to come first."

"Kane's not like that," Sasha said, realizing something new about Kane even as she said it. All along, she thought he was the safe choice because he wasn't like her. Because he had that ability to compartmentalize his emotions. The last few hours had put an end to that theory.

"Well, he should be. Guys who aren't don't live long in our business or they turn to the other side."

"The smart ones get out."

"Is that what you did?" he asked.

She was a little surprised that Temple had guessed she had been in the game. But she hadn't gotten out because of any rational thinking on her part. She'd gotten out because she'd faced her own dark side and it had scared her.

"If you did, why are you back?" Temple asked.

"I couldn't let Kane be brought in by..."

"Someone like me."

"Yes. You're angry at Kane and Kane's angry at the world."

Temple leaned back and studied her. "And there you are stuck in the middle."

"I'm not exactly stuck, Temple. I chose to be here."

"Are you sure about that?"

She nodded. But he'd raised doubts that she hadn't wanted to face. *Was* this where she belonged?

"So be it," Temple said and reached out for her arm. Before she could move, he had her arm twisted behind her back and her own weapon pressed under her chin.

"I think you'll help me now."

"I don't think so," she replied. She brought her knee up slightly and dug her heel into his instep.

Bruce groaned in pain and Sasha captured his wrist in both of her hands and swung around behind him. She twisted his arm behind his back. "I don't want to fight you, Bruce. I think we can find a similar objective here. Townsend needs to be stopped." If he wouldn't talk to her, he was going to be bound and gagged and left behind this rotting Dumpster.

He twisted in her grip, jerking hard on his arm until he could see her. "Kane going after him like some crazy man isn't going to help anyone."

Sasha kept a cautious eye on him. He stood maybe three feet away from her, rubbing his wrist. "Agreed. Can we talk?"

"Yes," he said.

Sasha didn't immediately holster her weapon. He eyed the Glock and her. "Trust has to start somewhere."

"You're still armed," she pointed out.

"Touché."

Bruce put his own gun away and turned toward the mouth of the alley. "There's a Häagen-Dazs around the corner. Let's go there."

"Okay." She followed him out of the alley, praying that Kane and Orly stayed wherever they were. In Temple's eyes she saw the same rage that burned inside her. A rage that stemmed from betrayal. If Bruce saw her husband now, he would probably react before she could reason with him.

They ordered ice cream and found a seat in the back of the store. Sasha toyed with the iced dessert, which she'd ordered in a cup, out of habit, so she could share it with Dylan.

"So talk," Temple said.

"I want you on our side. Townsend is wily but I think we can find him and bring Anna back without having to compromise anyone else."

"HMIA already proposed this and Sterling walked."

"I don't understand. What happened?"

"I don't know. And he's not talking." Though Kane never really discussed his work, he had mentioned that Bruce had one of the most logical minds Kane had ever met. She needed that on their side. They weren't going to stumble across Townsend simply because she'd been lucky enough to find him once before.

The last time she'd followed the signs that Perry had left for her. She doubted Anna would even think to do anything like that.

"Was it your boss's decision that set Kane off?" she asked. Kane's boss, Benjamin Shubert, was a tough but fair man. She'd worked with him before she met Kane and had a lot of respect for the man. He really cared not only about doing the job but also about keeping his men in top condition—mentally, emotionally and physically. Shubert would have understood that Kane was having a tough time accepting his sister's kidnapping.

Bruce took a sip of the milk shake he'd ordered.

"Actually, no. I think I was more upset than he was. He said that HMIA knew how to deal with madmen—especially ones they'd trained. He was willing to go along with Shubert's plan."

"When was Anna taken?" she asked, toying with the ice cream she had no desire to eat.

"Two days ago."

"So Kane was okay for what, about a day?"

"No, actually more like two. Then he said we had to act. Tossed his gun and badge at Shubert and walked out."

Sasha nodded. It was clear Kane was still hiding at least one secret. "Let me talk to Kane and find out what happened."

"I…hell, Sasha." Temple leaned forward, rubbing both of his eyes with the heels of hands. "Okay. But meet me at the town house by midnight. If you haven't gotten any information from him by then I'm taking him in, whatever it takes. If you get in my way…"

"Understood."

Temple nodded, stood and walked out of the store. Sasha watched him go. This wasn't what she'd expected when she'd returned to fieldwork. How long could she keep the balls she was juggling in the air? she wondered. How long could she manage to keep everyone happy? Would it be long enough to save Kane? She was no longer confident it would be. Her husband was not acting like the man she'd married and their closest friends were quickly turning to enemies.

A heavy hand fell on her shoulder and she looked up to see Orly standing beside her with Kane. Both men were out of place in the ice-cream store. Dark, brooding Kane looked like a marauder from long ago. Trendy, sexy Orly looked as if he was on his way to a SoHo nightclub. She glanced at her own jeans and a casual sweater and then compared that attire to that of the other patrons. She fit in here. She could go back to being Sasha Sterling.

Yet, in her heart, she knew she belonged with these two men. She was Nightshade, one of the best operatives ever in the field. She needed to remember that.

She handed the ice cream to Orly and he took it with a grin. "Let's go."

Orly led the way out of the shop.

"What did Temple want?" Kane asked softly.

"You, the chip and some sort of retribution."

"What'd you offer him?" Kane asked.

Sasha didn't respond. What was she going to say? That she agreed with Temple? That it was past time for Kane to leave off his vengeance and turn over the chip? He already knew that. He also knew that she'd made a choice, at least temporarily, to stay by his side.

"I'll get the car," Orly said.

"Did you find anything?"

"I'm not sure. The boys we spoke to remember the man who grabbed Anna because he had some cool ink on his neck."

"A tattoo of what?"

"They couldn't see the entire thing because of the man's collar but they sketched out this."

Kane handed her a napkin with a crude drawing on it. The drawing was a stylized gothic-looking cross with a grinning skull in the middle of it. She would've remembered that as well. She shivered a little as a breeze blew through the street.

Kane hesitated then wrapped his arm around her shoulder and drew her up against his side. His body warmth immediately permeated her clothing and the chills subsided. "This was a good idea."

"What was?"

"Investigating. I focused only on forcing him to give her back."

"But that's not going to work, is it? We have no way of contacting Townsend."

Kane said nothing.

"Do we?"

"He's contacted me twice now. I was supposed to get a location from those men on the dock tonight."

"A location for what?"

"To drop the list."

"Then I'm glad I stopped you because if I hadn't you'd be dead."

"I'm not sure of that," Kane said. Orly pulled to the curb. Kane opened the door of the BMW and Sasha slid across the seat. He followed her in the car and closed the door. Silence was their companion on their trip across town to the house they'd lived in during their unconventional courtship. Sasha couldn't think of anything to say in response. What wasn't Kane telling her?

The house was quiet when they got home. With Sasha assigned to Kane's retrieval other units had been taken off round the clock surveillance of his London residence. It had been over six months since Sasha had been there and yet nothing had changed. They'd dropped Orly at his place across town before making plans to meet later. Omar, Kane's butler, seemed surprised to see her but he was too well trained to comment.

"Omar, Mrs. Sterling will be staying with us for the next few weeks. Please ensure her room is ready."

Omar was a few inches shorter than Sasha and was dressed in a day suit. He had a passion for brightly colored ties and today's was a brilliant mango color. He smiled at her and Sasha smiled back. "It's a pleasure to see you again, Mrs. Sterling. Will Master Dylan be joining us as well?"

"Not right now," Kane said. "We'll be in the study. Please bring us in some coffee."

"Yes, sir."

"Thank you, Omar," Sasha said, watching the butler walk away.

Kane turned without a word and walked down the short hall into his study. The room was richly appointed with a deep cherry-wood desk and sideboard. One wall was lined with a floor-to-ceiling bookcase, another wall held a map of the world and awards that Kane had won over the years. A large picture window was on the third wall and offered a view of the small box garden in the backyard.

Kane took off his jacket as he entered the room, tossing it on the brocade love seat. She shed her leather jacket as well. When Kane turned, she saw his holster at the small of his back. She'd debated letting him have his weapon and in the end, fear for his safety had forced her to let him keep it.

He rolled up the sleeves on his black silk shirt and then went to his desk. Sasha hovered indecisively. He glanced up at her, his thick dark hair rakishly disheveled from the wind. "Say what you have to say."

Coward, she thought. But the truth of the matter was that facing an armed assailant was infinitely less nerve-racking than having this conversation with Kane. "I'm not sure where to start."

"At the beginning," he said in a wry tone that was very reminiscent of the old Kane.

"I have a few questions."

He raised one eyebrow, inviting her to go on. She realized that the way they were situated gave Kane the power. He was sitting in his big leather executive chair and she was standing in front of his desk like some subordinate who was being called on the carpet.

"It's about something Temple said," she said.

"Go ahead and ask, Sasha. If I don't want to answer, I won't."

She crossed the room and, propping her hip on the corner of the desk, she stared into his icy gray eyes. Now that she was seated higher than Kane, she felt she'd taken back the power. "What happened with Shubert? Bruce said you were willing to follow procedures at first."

Kane leaned back in his chair, stretching his long jean-clad legs out in front of him. Sasha thought he wasn't going to respond. If he didn't, she was going to have to take him in to Ano. She couldn't help him find Anna and apprehend Townsend unless she had the entire story.

"When Anna was snatched, Townsend delivered his ransom notice to HMIA before Mother even knew Anna was gone. It was almost two hours before she was notified that Anna had been abducted."

"That must have been frustrating." What an understatement. She imagined Kane trying to verify that his kid sister had been taken by a man with a huge vendetta against the very agency he worked for. Sasha knew from personal experience that when your job endangered your loved ones, it put you in a spot that was beyond uncomfortable.

Kane nodded. "Well, Townsend knows that HMIA doesn't negotiate with kidnappers. And he also knew we'd immediately start watching airports, train stations and ports.

"Shubert assigned two agents to the case. He offered me a temporary leave, which I declined."

"Why?" Sasha asked. What she really wanted to know was why he hadn't called her. It was obvious that he needed a shoulder to lean on.

Kane pushed away from the desk, stood and paced to the window. He stared out at the backyard for a long time. She didn't think he was going to answer. Then he did, his voice rusty and devoid of emotion.

"I needed to work. When I came home that first night…let's just say we both know too much about what happens to victims."

"Why didn't you call me, Kane?" Sasha asked, not realizing she was going to.

"We're separated," he said curtly.

Sasha went to his side and still he didn't turn and look at her. "By your choice. I would've come to London."

He rubbed his jaw and glanced at her. "Actually, that's why I didn't call you. The next morning I had an e-mail from Townsend that suggested he'd negotiate with me if I brought the STAR list to him. I declined, of course.

"That afternoon I realized someone was following me, and I knew if you came to London with Dylan, you'd both be in danger."

She understood that Dylan's safety was a foremost concern for Kane. Losing his sister was bad enough, he wasn't going to give Townsend another victim. That made sense. Kane was being drawn between doing what he wanted to do, using his lethal skills for retribution and his own conscience. She'd been there and knew just how difficult a place that was. Whatever decision he made, he had to live with the what-ifs and could-have-beens. It wasn't an easy place to be. And Sasha didn't know if she could help Kane navigate that area. While she wanted to wrap her arms around him and offer him the comfort of her body, she also knew that once she let her own emotions free she'd be in the same position Kane was in. And they couldn't afford that.

"Why did Townsend contact you?"

"I'm not sure. But he's done so twice. I went to Shubert and asked for the list.

"He flat out said no. Hell, I don't blame him." Kane turned away from her again.

She looked at this man who'd done something she couldn't really comprehend. She'd left the Agency and gone out on her own but she'd never put anyone save herself in jeopardy. "Yet you took it."

"I had no choice. Townsend backed me into a corner and he knew it. Shubert is acting, but things are moving too slowly through proper channels. Anna will be dead before Shubert gets to Townsend…he wants enough evidence to prosecute."

"Why?"

"They're old enemies. Shubert had been Townsend's partner for years."

"I didn't realize that. I thought Townsend was angry at his superior."

"Shubert *is* that superior. He got a promotion Townsend thought should have been his."

"So what's Townsend after now? Your downfall or Shubert's?"

"I don't care," Kane said. "I just want to bring my sister home and make that son of a bitch pay."

Chapter 7

Praise and blame, gain and loss, pleasure and
sorrow come and go like the wind.

—Achaan Chaa

Sasha left Kane in his study and went to the room
that had always been hers. There was a connecting
door that led to Kane's bedroom. Actually, the door
to the bedroom that they had always shared. She
knew she wouldn't be sharing it tonight.

She'd be out gathering clues. So far, Kane hadn't
said anything that indicated he was going to surrender the STAR list to anyone. Kane was holding the
fate of every agent in his hands. The list was a major
stumbling block. Until that was retrieved and returned, Kane was going to be battling Townsend and

other foes that used to be friends. And she realized that she didn't totally trust him.

She put on a CD of Mozart and closed her eyes. Letting the magic of "A Little Night Music" wash over her. She calmed her mind, shedding the day's worries and concentrating on Anna. The girl would be worth a lot for Townsend to keep alive. At least until he got the list. Still, they'd have to be careful not to piss him off. Sasha used her cell phone to scheduled appointments for tomorrow with the three friends that Anna had been shopping with when she'd been abducted.

The list circled back into her mind. She needed to find it. Perhaps Kane had hidden it here. Cautiously she opened his bedroom door intent on searching the room. She hovered on the doorstep, halfway in, and halfway to taking a step that would put an even bigger rift between her and Kane.

She glanced around the room. His bed was made, but the servants probably took care of that. On his nightstand was a picture of her and Dylan. She froze. Staring at the picture of herself and their son.

The fact that she hesitated told her she wasn't going to take the chip from Kane. She'd just have to make sure that he didn't get it to Townsend. Decision made, she turned around and reentered her room, closing the door firmly behind her. Kane was standing inside her bedroom watching her.

Something electric passed between them. An innate awareness that trust had been broken arced through the room. Sasha wanted to say something to explain but words just wouldn't come.

"I…"

He rubbed the bridge between his eyes. Did he have a headache? Kane was plagued with them usually only when he was working on an intense case. She took a step toward him, intent on massaging his neck and bringing him some relief.

"You don't need to explain," he said. "Charity is waiting downstairs. She has some information from the men we captured."

She crossed her arms over her chest, feeling small and alone. Something she'd felt many times in the past but not recently. There was something about being a mom that meant she didn't have to be alone. But now she was. She rubbed her hands over her arms and then dropped them.

"Great. I'll be right down."

Kane pivoted on his heel. Suddenly she couldn't watch him walk away again. Sure, she knew that he was just going downstairs, but it felt as if he was leaving again, and she wasn't going to watch him go.

"Kane?"

He paused but didn't turn around. Instead, he glanced back over his shoulder, watching her with inscrutable eyes, and she felt the lies between them. Lies that he hadn't spoken yet but would soon. Felt all that hadn't been said and still needed to be. Felt as if she never should have left Dylan in Leeds. Felt that she never should have allowed Kane to leave without letting him realize that he was a necessary part of their family.

"Yes, Sasha?"

She ached for all that needed to be said. For words that had nothing to do with the case and his current actions. Words that would make him understand that he was still the only man she wanted in her life.

"Nothing. Let's go meet Charity," Sasha said, walking around Kane and leading the way downstairs. With each step she took, she distanced herself from Sasha—wife and mother—and made herself into Nightshade. It was night, and time for her to do what she'd been trained for.

Find a young girl and stop a criminal mastermind from succeeding in his plot to ruin the intelligence community.

Kane led the way downstairs and into his office. Charity was waiting for them. She wore a pair of camel-colored trousers, a silky black shirt and a matching blazer. She gave Sasha a questioning look when she entered that Sasha ignored.

"What'd you find out?" she asked Charity. Sasha wasn't going to be the second on this case. She was in charge and she'd make damn sure that both of them knew it.

Charity handed Sasha a typed transcript of the interrogation and Sasha scanned it while Charity talked. "The men were hired to take Kane."

"Tell us something we don't know, Charity," Kane said. He'd crossed the room and was leaning against his desk.

"How do I know what information *you* have?" Charity demanded in that supersweet tone of hers that Sasha knew meant her friend was minutes away from losing her temper.

"Townsend's been contacting him," Sasha said, to alleviate the battle she sensed was brewing.

"Why?" Charity asked Kane.

"Why do you think? The price for Anna's life is that list."

"The chances of Townsend actually letting both you and Anna leave alive are very slim," Charity said.

"I'm not an idiot," he said.

"Just act like one, huh?"

"Enough," Sasha said. "According to this document the men were contacted at a nightclub in SoHo."

"Which one?"

"Café de Paris on Coventry."

"Keep up the good work, Charity. Let us know if you find out anything else."

"I won't have to let you know. I'm going with you."

"What?"

"Ano's orders. I'm your shadow until that list is returned to HMIA."

Sasha knew that Ano was giving her a chance to do this her way and she appreciated her boss's confidence in her. "Okay, let's get ready for a night on the town."

Sasha paused outside Café de Paris. Ano had sent over clothes from Mango, a Spanish fashion house that dressed the hip and trendy. Sasha liked wearing the clothes, and the illusion of unreality came again as she and Kane made their way to the front of the line.

Justice and Charity were also dressed to the nines, and all four of them blended into the well-heeled crowd of the club.

The white pants and black cardigan trimmed in white made her feel less like a mom and more like a woman who was made for the nightlife. Sliding back into her agent skin was second nature. Sliding back into this kind of lifestyle was something else. She'd never really been that comfortable with the scene to begin with. She zipped the cardigan to a spot right between her breasts. Making her cleavage look bigger than it actually was.

Her retro black-and-white handbag held her Glock, lipstick and Blackberry cell phone.

"Come on, Sasha. The night's wasting away," Kane said.

His wardrobe didn't need any sprucing up. Kane had the kind of style that Sasha envied. Dolce & Gabbana had made the white shirt and jeans he wore. He'd pulled on a black tuxedo jacket over the ensemble and a pair of Bruno Magli black laced shoes.

"Why are you so anxious to go inside?" she asked. Using their contacts at A.R.C., Sasha had made a reservation for a drinking table in the Blue Bar close to the main dance floor.

"Two reasons," he said. That charming rogue was in his smile, and her heart beat a little faster. "One—the key to finding Anna might be in there."

"I know that. What's two?" she asked.

"It's been a long time since I held you in my arms," he said. This was the real problem between them. Outside of work there was no connection. No common ground. They didn't know each other away from the danger, and even parenthood hadn't brought them much closer.

And yet a shiver of pure sensual awareness snaked through Sasha. God, she hadn't felt this way since she'd brought Dylan home from the hospital. This wasn't the way she wanted to be going into a dangerous mission. She needed stoicism. She needed to be the fearless and much-feared Nightshade. Instead, she was Sasha—wife, mother, ball of emotional uncertainty.

Kane was staring at her.

"Who's fault is that?" she asked him.

"Are we really going to start the blame game?" he asked. That softness that had been in his eyes just a minute ago was now gone.

She wanted things both ways. She wanted Kane to be totally devoted to her and still accept whatever she was willing to give him. "No. I've missed it too."

Charity, Justice and Orly were providing backup. Orly in the Rover parked in a back alley. And Charity was already inside with Justice, checking out the joint. They all had voice-activated communication devices and an earpiece. They'd all be in contact. Which was one reason why she'd agreed to let Kane come with them. Who was she kidding? She'd never have been able to keep Kane at home no matter what she tried.

She and Kane were the last of the players to arrive. Now came the time to pony up the trust. She was going to have to leave Kane alone—to show him that she trusted him, because Townsend wasn't going to approach Kane while anyone was standing next to him.

Kane put his hand at her waist and urged her toward the door. The bouncer took one look at Kane, smiled at him and let them in.

"How does he know you?" she asked, realizing that she was a little jealous. She'd been staying home with Dylan, and Kane had been in London. Had he been doing more than just working?

"This is where Townsend sent me the first time," Kane said. There was something in his eyes that said he knew what she'd been thinking.

"Oh."

"I still consider myself a married man," he said quietly.

"Let's talk about that later. What did you get from Townsend?"

"The picture of Anna."

Kane said little else weaving his way through the throng of people just inside the doorway. Tonight the music was a mix of disco house and funk. The years were stripped away and she was back in her early twenties when she'd practically lived in clubs. Hell, they all had in those days. Working their asses off in agent training and partying the nights away. It had been a carefree time.

They approached the hostess and confirmed their reservation. They were seated at a two-top table near the dance floor. The steel-blue interior and rich electric-blue carpet was crowded.

"What do you want to drink?" Kane asked.

She'd never been able to hold her liquor. She worked much better with a clear focus and nothing inhibiting her senses. "I'd love a French martini, but I'm not sure I should drink."

Kane leaned over, the scent of his aftershave filling her senses. He brushed his mouth along her cheek and then bit the lobe of her ear. He skimmed one long lean finger down the side of her face. "We don't want anyone to know we're working."

The words were warm and hot, spoken right into her ear, and carried no farther than she. She'd forgotten the most elemental of rules. Maybe it was too late to be back in this game. She turned her face, brushed her lips against his jaw and then pulled back. "I meant because I haven't had a drink since I had the baby."

He nodded and signaled the waitress, ordering her drink and a vodka martini for himself. "Want to dance?"

Kane took her hand and led her through the crowd to the dance floor. They danced for fifteen minutes before Orly noticed some activity behind the club.

"Black BMW just pulled up and the man with the cane from the docks stepped out. He's wearing a tailored suit and has two bodyguard types with him. They look like the guys you took down last night."

"Gotcha," Sasha said.

"I'll take care of this," Kane said, leading her off the dance floor back toward their table. The long, low, padded blue bench near their table was crowded with people engaged in conversation.

"They know you. What were your instructions the last time?"

"To go to one of the VIP rooms."

"Where are they located?"

"Off the main room through a discreet door. Your name has to be on the list."

"Not a problem."

"Big problem. I don't want your name on any list that Townsend might get hold of."

"Because of Dylan?"

"Yes, and because you're my wife. I take care of my own."

"I'm not exactly helpless," she said.

"My mind knows that, Sasha, but my gut…hell, I'm more primitive male than you'd be comfortable with."

"I like that primitive side."

"Stop flirting, Nightshade. I've identified the man from the docks as Hans von Buren. He's an import/export man from Berlin," Orly said.

They were seated at their table. Each took a sip of their drinks. Then Sasha leaned in close to Kane and they twined their hands together and gazed into each other's eyes, giving the appearance of two people totally absorbed with each other. They spoke softly to the team.

"Kane's name is on the list for tonight," Charity said.

"Did you know that?" Sasha asked him.

"I bet it's on there every night."

"Checking," Orly said. "Confirmed. Kane's

name has been on the list every night since Anna disappeared."

"I'm going into the VIP room and get some answers," Kane said.

"Don't do anything too violent."

"No promises."

"Be sensible. We can tail von Buren."

"I'll keep it in mind," Kane said. He let go of Sasha's hands and finished his martini. He stood, then leaned down and kissed her. It was a deeply carnal kiss that rocked her to her soul. Then he walked away. And she found that she couldn't watch him leave.

She sipped her French martini and brooded. Kane was at times reminding her of the man she fell in love with and an operative that she'd always respected while still being a man she wasn't sure had ever loved her back. As well as being a rogue agent who could destroy what many had spent a long time building.

"What's your plan?" Orly asked.

Sasha turned the situation over in her head. No time to worry about Kane. They needed to be able to follow von Buren when he left. One car—especially one like the Land Rover—was going to stand out. They needed to plant a tracking device either in his car or on the man.

"What kind of beacons do we have?" she asked. She wasn't going to rely on Kane. Was von Buren the man Kane was supposed to meet?

"Checking."

"Sterling, is von Buren your contact?"

"Negative. Never saw him until the docks."

"Gotcha. Are you in the VIP room yet?"

"Yes. Will contact you later."

"Affirmative," Nightshade said. Kane was in total work mode. His voice was low, of course, but also devoid of emotion. That reassured her. Because he sounded more in control of himself.

"Justice, can you slow VB down to give me some time to figure out a plan?"

"I'm on it," Justice said. Sasha scanned the room. The music had changed and a new deejay had taken over. The new music had more of a punk feel to it. The beat rocked through the club and through Sasha. She wanted to come back here again, she thought. Not all the time, but maybe once in a while. Once this mission was complete. Once everything was settled.

"Charity, meet me in the ladies' room."

"Gotcha."

Sasha finished her drink and tossed a few bills on the table to cover the tab in case she didn't get back. She made her way to the rest room. There was an attendant, and Sasha used the facility. She debated moving the Glock from her purse to a holster at the small of her back. But a gun in a crowded nightclub was a recipe for disaster, so she left it in her purse. She had other ways of defending herself if she needed to.

She washed her hands and mingled with Charity at the makeup mirror, both of them touching up their lipstick. There was a small cluster of women gossiping about the men they'd come with. They were slim and sophisticated, but they reminded Sasha of the group of new moms she met with at the park every Wednesday morning. And in that moment she realized that despite the trappings of singlehood or marriage, women's groups were largely the same. They provided a special kind of camaraderie. "Can we get close enough to plant whatever Orly finds?"

"No problem."

"I've got a business card that's been wired with a microscopic transmission beacon." Cutting-edge technology was one of the reasons that American Renegade Company was used frequently by so many government agencies. Ano made sure the latest-and-greatest gear and gadgets were tested and vetted and available.

"Sounds good. Be at the velvet rope," Nightshade said.

"Gotcha."

Charity ran her fingers through her hair, fluffing it up a bit. "I'll help Justice keep him occupied and then pass on my card."

The two women left the bathroom. Von Buren had finally made it to the main dance floor. Tonight he didn't have a cane with him. His two bodyguards were providing a moving barrier around him.

"You read my mind," Nightshade said.

"It's not that hard to do since we were both trained by the same diabolical one."

"Be careful or I might tell your mom."

Charity threw her head back and laughed in a way that drew the stares of many men in the room. Sasha wondered why her friend hadn't settled down, but she knew Charity preferred to play the singles scene.

Justice was talking to von Buren, but he had noticed Charity was wearing a skintight blue halter dress. Charity had worked as a catwalk model for three years before returning to A.R.C. And she still had the ability to pull that sexy walk and sultry aura off with ease. Sasha never had the ability. She admired her friend even as she pushed past Charity to head toward the main entrance. She spotted Orly with his blue-tipped spiked hair talking to the bouncer and comparing deejays.

He didn't seem to move and Sasha knew that the bouncer didn't even notice when Orly twitched his fingers and Sasha took the spy card from him.

She pivoted and made her way back into the club. The crowd was growing. Sasha weaved her way through the talking and drinking people. She couldn't find von Buren, Charity or Justice.

She could hear them both chatting with von Buren, though. The man spoke English with a faint accent. The sounds of the deejay were muted and Sasha scanned the club, still unable to find them.

"I need directions," Sasha said.

"I've never been up to the mezzanine level before. I usually just spend my time on the dance floor," Justice said.

"I'll bet you do," von Buren purred.

"Thanks." Sasha left the main area and headed for the mezzanine. It took her a few minutes to get up there. The low couches and underlit glass tables of the mezzanine area were full.

The lively music and party atmosphere was so foreign to her that she moved through it as an observer. She was definitely more interested in play-dates than the club scene. Though the music did move that deep jungle feeling inside her.

She slowed even more, letting the beat rule her steps. Her hips just swayed naturally to the music. This she missed. She worked her way through the room. When she moved closer to the table where Justice, Charity and von Buren were, she saw Charity's small clutch purse on the floor near her feet.

She took a deep breath and prayed that her aim would be accurate and true, and as she sashayed past the table, she opened her fingers and dropped the card into the open purse.

The hardest temptation was to not look back and see if she'd actually hit it. But then the way she was feeling, she couldn't have missed.

Chapter 8

Let us not look back in anger or forward in fear,
but around in awareness.

—James Thurber

Nightshade continued through the mezzanine level.
She saw a familiar face in the crowd at the bar.
Looking casual and a little out of place was Bruce
Temple.

"Temple's in the house," she sang softly.

"Keep him out of my way, Nightshade."

"Gotcha, Sterling."

Walking on the balls of her feet so that her heels
didn't make a sound, Nightshade snaked around behind Temple and wrapped one arm around his waist

and leaned on the bar with the other. Effectively trapping him unless he wanted to make a scene.

"I thought we agreed to meet at midnight."

"I couldn't wait," he said. Then in a tone that was so low it only reached her ears, "I wasn't sure whose team you were on," he said. A dark anger burned in his eyes.

Feeling like a fire juggler at Cirque du Soleil trying desperately not to get burned, she said, "Don't make this difficult."

"I'm not the one who did," he said smoothly. "Want a drink?"

"French martini."

He signaled the bartender and ordered for both of them. Sasha perched on the stool next to him. "This isn't the place for us to talk."

"I'm not leaving until Sterling does."

The electric music spinning below them was loud, but filtered through the sound of talking voices. She heard the base line for Coldplay's "Clocks." And deliberately tuned the music out, but the lyric echoed in her head.

"Sasha?"

"I'm sorry, Bruce. Did you say something?"

"Your drink arrived."

Her pinkish martini was sitting at her elbow. She lifted the glass toward Temple. He clinked his shot glass against it and said, "Cheers."

She sipped, letting the mixture of Chambord, vodka and pineapple juice linger on her tongue before swallowing. People were smoking in the club and

Sasha closed her eyes. It was easy to pretend she was somewhere else. Fatigue washed over her in a wave.

"You're burning the candle at both ends. Go back home where you belong."

"I am where I belong, Temple. You're the only one who shouldn't be here."

"I'm not leaving. Listen, there are players in this game that you might not be aware of. I won't let you jeopardize everything."

"You'll have to trust me," Nightshade said. There just wasn't time to debate with Temple. "Let's go."

"I'm serious, Sasha."

"So am I. For the sake of the friendship you and Kane have had for so long, please believe me now."

Temple stared at her for so long she thought he wasn't going to give in, but then he sighed and stood up.

"I'll be at the town house at midnight and I'll want answers."

Relief knifed through her. She didn't want to have to keep fighting people she knew and cared for. "You'll get them. We might be a little later."

"Why?"

"I'm going to tail someone." Temple didn't need to know too many details. He'd made it clear he was only after the STAR list.

"On foot?"

"We're hoping to use an electronic burr."

"Who's we?"

Sasha couldn't start naming names. She didn't want to expose any of them in case Temple decided to take the information back to HMIA. Ano and the entire Renegade team would be in trouble then. "I…"

"I'm supposed to trust you but you aren't going to trust me?" Temple asked sarcastically.

"You're not sure you do, remember? I can't take a chance."

"All right. Listen, I can't just sit around. Let me help you with your surveillance." There was a look in Temple's eyes that underscored those words.

Sasha debated for about a minute then said, "One minute, Temple. Orly, you there?"

"Go ahead, Nightshade."

"I'm sending Temple out to meet you. Arrange to follow our man when he leaves."

"Gotcha."

"There's a black Land Rover parked on Lisle Street. Orly will brief you on a need-to-know basis."

"Dylan's nanny." Temple and Orly were always going at each other.

"Blimey, Sasha, tell that prick I'm not a nanny. I'm a bodyguard."

"He's a bodyguard," Nightshade said to Temple.

Bruce stood and left the bar. Nightshade pretended to finish her drink, keeping a judicious eye on the room. "Sterling, how're things where you are?"

There was no answer. "Sterling?"

Still nothing. Maybe they were having a technical glitch. "Everyone check in."

"Orly here."

"Justice here. Charity can't check in but she's here."

"Nightshade here."

Nothing from Kane. Dammit. "Orly, check where-abouts of Sterling, please."

Their wireless mike/earpieces also served as tracking devices. If he'd disappeared, she was going to find him and put him in cuffs and turn him over to A.R.C. What did he think he was doing?

"He should still be in the VIP room."

"Gotcha, Orly. I'm going to do a visual."

"Gotcha."

Sasha left the bar and returned to the main level where the Blue Bar was. She made her way to the back where the door to the VIP rooms were. The guard on duty was tall, and it was obvious from the fit of his jacket that he'd spent a lot of time lifting weights. Nightshade paused and waited until he spotted her.

She caught his eye, smiled briefly then looked away. A few minutes later she glanced back at him. He was still watching her. She walked toward him, smiling a little the entire time.

Two hours later Sasha was back at A.R.C. head-quarters. The computer room where they'd congregated was dimly lit. There were banks of computer terminals on one wall and a large map of the world. They'd plugged in the coordinates for von Buren's tracker and Orly's vehicle. So they could track them both.

Pissed as hell at her husband. Though she'd never admit it, she was also scared for him. He was playing a game that couldn't be won, and until he stopped giving her the slip, she couldn't help him.

Temple and Orly were on von Buren, trailing him to find out where he was going and see if maybe he was meeting with Townsend. Sasha, Charity and Justice had returned to headquarters to track down her elusive husband once more.

Ano hadn't put in an appearance yet and Sasha hoped she didn't. Confronting her boss when she'd just lost not only the STAR list but also the only lead they had in finding Anna wasn't something she was ready to do.

Sinking deeper into her armed-leather chair, she studied the monitor in front of her. She'd put Hans von Buren into the database and though he skated on the edge of the law he'd never been linked to anything criminal. He'd been born in Berlin during the cold war. His father had been a government man who'd died while Hans was in college. Hans started his own business in the late 1980s and had been successfully importing and exporting cheap goods from Asia into Europe since.

"What's the connection?" she asked out loud. Most of von Buren's time had been spent setting up trade with Asia.

"I don't know," Charity said. She crossed her arms and leaned against the countertop. "From our conversations he's definitely successful and funny."

"Bad guys can't be funny?" Justice asked in that sarcastic way of hers. She had taken a seat next to Sasha and was working at her own computer terminal. Justice was pure magic with a computer and had solved many crimes from her small workstation while other agents beat the street for clues. It wasn't that she accessed databases or information the rest of them didn't. It was the questions she asked. Justice looked at the world differently.

She'd grown up on the street and she had a low opinion of everyone. It took a long time to ease her doubts and an even longer time to gain her trust. Sasha wasn't sure she ever entirely had.

"Of course they can be funny."

"What else did you get from him, Charity?"

"He loves his grandkids. He must have mentioned them three times while we were having drinks."

"He's especially proud of the son—Otto?" Justice said.

Sasha punched the name into the database and stats came back a few seconds later. Otto von Buren, a twenty-two-year-old graduate student who was making strides in the field of cloning. "I'd be proud too."

"So what's the verdict?" Sasha asked. "Is he connected to Townsend?"

"His partner from the other night, Larry Tanner, is definitely working for Townsend. We've identified him as the man who delivered the first ransom demand to Kane."

"So there is a connection. Is there any other reason these two men would be together?"

Justice reached over Sasha and pulled up a file. "Tanner and von Buren both work on the docks. Von Buren keeps an office there that he visits once a month to check his goods coming in from Asia and other parts of the world. Tanner's job is dockmaster, so there is a legitimate reason for them to be together. But…"

"We don't believe in coincidences," the three women said at the same time.

That was the first lesson they'd learned when they'd been accepted into A.R.C. and started their training. Just about every brief they'd ever been given started with that line.

They all smiled at each other. For a light moment it wasn't much, but Sasha savored it. She wasn't alone. She had to remember that. There was much to be said for working with her friends. For figuring out the case together. She wished Kane was here and could see what she did. That going it alone helped no one.

"I have an idea," Sasha said. She punched in a wild-card search for von Buren and Townsend. She asked the computer to access the cases Townsend had worked on as an agent for HMIA as well as all his suspected activities when he left the Agency.

Slowly information started pouring in. But it didn't filter out anything that had the two men together. "Justice, any ideas?"

"Let me take the driver's seat."

Sasha stood and let Justice take her seat. She paced over to the map with the flashing lights that showed Orly and von Buren, or von Buren's bug had stopped moving.

Sasha let the sounds of Justice's keyboard clicking soothe the troubles of her mind. But it didn't work. Anxiety—no, worry—for Kane was making it impossible to distance herself from the case. A large wave of black emotion started deep in her stomach and rolled up the back of her throat. Threatening to choke her.

Closing her eyes, she forced herself to breathe deeply. Suddenly she grappled for the one thing that made her feel good—really good. Dylan. His little face winked into her mind's eye and she used the overwhelming feelings of love and protectiveness she felt toward him to batten down the rage that threatened to consume her.

"Nightshade, I think I found something."

Sasha hurried across the room and leaned over the back of the chair to stare at the computer screen. She skimmed the article that Justice had pulled up. It wasn't much really, barely even worth mentioning, but Elias Townsend's son, Paul, and Hans von Buren's son, Otto, had attended prep school together.

Sasha left A.R.C. headquarters a little after midnight. Justice, Charity and Nightshade had played with the variables and the players until they'd realized they were chasing their tail. Justice was working on the computer and they'd made plans to meet in the morning to discuss their findings.

One of the operatives had gone to retrieve Sasha's Aston so she'd be able to drive it home. Her mind set to autopilot, she drove effortlessly through the streets of London. She played the variables of the case over in her mind. She knew that the clock was ticking. Knew that time was winding faster and faster toward an ending she had no control over.

Nightshade still had to meet with Temple tonight, and his realizing she'd lost Kane wasn't going to make him want to stay a team player. Also, she wasn't exactly sure what Temple's agenda was. Ano hadn't been able to figure it out either. She'd advised Sasha to get whatever information she could from Temple without revealing anything that they knew.

She rubbed the bridge of her nose, acknowledging that this was why she'd gotten out of the business. She'd forgotten what it was like not to be able to trust anyone.

She wanted to talk to her little boy. To pull him into her arms and assure herself that he was safe. She checked the clock and then dialed her dad's cell number.

"Malone."

"It's me."

"What's up, kiddo?" he asked in that gruff voice of his that always reassured her. It was his middle-of-the-night voice and had kept more than one nightmare at bay when she'd been a girl.

What was up? She knew something was wrong inside. Something that she'd wrapped tightly to protect herself was coming unwound and she didn't know how to get it back in the wrapping. "I'm just checking on Dylan."

"You can't fool me, kiddo. You called three hours ago and sang him to sleep."

"That's right, Dad. I can't fool you." How about myself? She didn't ask him though. Because she knew the answer. The time for fooling herself was over. She'd trusted Kane. And he'd betrayed her. In a very public way.

She took a deep breath. Her plan, which hadn't been all that firm, was undergoing a rapid change. Kane was definitely a hostile operative and, despite what she'd thought she knew about him, she was going to have to really take him when she found him again. "If Kane shows up or calls, I need to know."

"What's going on?"

"He disappeared tonight." Betrayal ripped through her. She'd done her share of finessing and escaping from other operatives before. In fact, she'd had to physically fight her way out of headquarters when she'd gone after Caroline's killers. But she'd never realized how it had felt to be the duped agent. The one left holding the bag.

"Dammit."

"I know. I didn't expect it. I should have."

He didn't say anything. Sasha felt her recriminations double. Her dad had trained her better than that. "Listen, keep Dylan close. I don't like the way this is playing out."

"What have you got?" he asked.

Not a hell of a lot. Just a few coincidences and some circumstantial stuff. But luckily they weren't going to have to prove their case in a court of law. "Just a couple of businessmen and second-generation friends. It might be nothing but I'm not sure."

"If things get hairy, I'll go to ground and contact when it's safe."

"If things get that bad, go to Georgia and I'll come get D when everything's clear."

"Roger that. I've been monitoring your business calls. Want me to cover the Jones contract for you?"

The Jones contract was the installation of a simple twenty-four-hour security setup with black-and-white monitors in the main office. Callie Jones had a daughter Dylan's age and had recommended Sasha to her husband. Brad Jones owned a novelty shop that was doing a good business but had been broken into three months ago.

"Sure. Bring Callie when you go in and she'll help you watch Dylan."

"Will do."

They rang off. Sasha arrived home and parked her car. Had Temple made it back yet?

Sasha picked up her two-way mike. "Orly?"

"I'm here."

"Still following von Buren?"

"Affirmative. It seems he's gone home for the night. I'm going to stay on the street and keep an eye on him."

"Want someone to spell you?"

"I'm good until 6:00 a.m. but we should probably have a different vehicle then."

"Gotcha. I'll get Ano to send you someone. I've got a meeting with Justice and Charity at eight and then interviews with Anna's friends at eleven. Get some sleep and meet me at A.R.C. headquarters this afternoon."

"Will do." Orly said.

"Is Temple still with you?" she asked.

"He left about ten minutes ago."

"Gotcha."

"Orly, relay the address and other pertinent details to Justice online…she's doing some computer legwork."

"My favorite kind."

Sasha smiled for the first time that night. "I know. Maybe you two can compare notes."

"Will do. Have you found Kane?"

"I'm not looking yet." Sasha replied firmly.

"Want to talk?"

"Have I ever?" she asked. She was the team leader and Orly's superior. It was never a good idea to whine about personal problems. She preferred to always let Orly believe she knew what she was doing.

"Later, boss lady."

Sasha gathered her things and climbed out of the car. Just as she fitted her key in the lock, a man stepped out of the shadows. Sasha dropped her jacket and pulled her gun an instant before she recognized Bruce Temple.

Chapter 9

We think in eternity, but we move slowly
through time.

—Oscar Wilde

"This was your idea," he said in that wry way of
his. He held his hands at his shoulders, clearly showing her he was unarmed. The night was cool and she
felt the chill through her sweater.

"I know. I was expecting you." She had also been
expecting Kane or any of his enemies. Because one
thing was becoming clear to her. Anna Sterling
hadn't been a random target. Townsend was going
after Kane, big-time. And that meant his house would
be watched.

"You're a little jumpy."

Sasha shrugged. "Considering the circumstances, I wasn't sure who I'd find. Come inside."

She finished unlocking the door and went to the alarm keypad once she'd stepped into the foyer. The alarm wasn't set. Sasha made a mental note of that fact and reset it. Was Kane in the house now? Or had he been here?

Omar came down the stairs. "Evening, Mrs. Sterling. Will you require anything?"

"I'm fine, Omar. Is Mr. Sterling home?" she asked.

Temple stiffened beside her. Torn, Sasha wished she'd never invited him to their home.

"No, ma'am."

He turned and went back upstairs. Sasha led the way through the quiet house to the small kitchen. She put on a pot of coffee. Temple came up behind her and massaged her neck with steady sure fingers. Sasha closed her eyes.

"You don't belong here," Temple said softly. "Tell me what you know and go back to your son."

A part of her agreed totally with Bruce. But another part, that secret hidden part that she was half-afraid of, disagreed. This was where she was most alive. This was what she'd been called to do. This was the only place she could be until she got her husband back.

She stepped away from him and took a seat by the small table. Temple watched her and she knew he was trying to decide which course of action to take. Seduction clearly wasn't going to work. Sasha didn't want any man but Kane. She hadn't realized that until right now.

"What'd you and Orly find out tonight?" she asked. The coffee finished brewing and she poured a cup for each of them, adding cream to hers. Temple took his black.

"Not much. Von Buren went straight home after he left the club. We didn't spot any other tails. Tell me about von Buren," Temple said. He sipped his coffee and leaned back in his chair. Very much the agent in charge.

"Tell me what you know," Sasha countered. She wasn't sharing any of the intelligence they'd gathered until she knew what Bruce had figured out.

"Are we really going to play this kind of game?" he asked silkily. He leaned forward and the kitchen light reflected off his blond hair.

"I don't know. Are you on our team?" she asked.

"Who's on the team?" he countered.

Sasha mulled it over for a minute and realized she either had to pony up some information or forget about getting anything from Temple. They were both too well trained. They could play this question and nonanswer game forever. "Renegade Company."

He quirked one eyebrow at her. "I'd always suspected you worked for them."

"Why?" she asked, because as far as she knew, there was nothing similar about any of the Company's agents. They were each unique and different. They each specialized in different weapons and different skills. They each used different tactics. How could Temple take one look at her and suspect A.R.C.?

He shrugged. Reaching across the table, he took her hand in his and stroked his finger across her wrist. "The way you move."

"Temple, stop."

"What?" he asked.

"Seduction is never going to work," she said bluntly. Fatigue weighed on her—she needed sleep. She needed answers and her temper was hanging by a thread. One more evasion and she was going to pin Temple to the floor and get her answers the hard way.

"How about sympathy, will that work?" he asked, dropping her hand.

She shook her head. Nothing but the truth would work, and the deeper she got on this case the harder the truth was to uncover. She took another sip of her coffee.

"Roughing you up?" he asked.

"Bring it on. I lost Kane and I'm ready to take my frustration out on someone."

He sat up straighter, all of his smooth moves gone. There was an intensity in his eyes that scared her for Kane's sake. "You lost Kane. Where?"

Sasha thought about keeping it secret but she knew at this point even Ano no longer trusted her to be the only one looking for Kane. And dammit, that made her mad. The man had chosen once again to be on his own instead of believing her. "Café de Paris. While you and I were talking."

"Any idea where he went?" Temple asked.

"Nope. I do know that von Buren is the man that Kane met the first time. He met him in a VIP room at the club," Sasha said. Maybe something would trigger Temple and he'd reveal any information he had.

"Kane brought you all there tonight?"

Sasha didn't say anything. Kane kept his cards very close to the chest, as doubtless Temple knew. She realized Kane had been playing her all along.

"No. We kind of put the pieces together as we went. Did you know about the club or follow us there?"

Temple leaned back in the chair, not speaking, but she could tell from the way he was watching her that he was weighing his options, trying to decide what information he should reveal. And what secrets were worth more if he kept them.

"I knew about the club. I went there with Kane the day Anna was taken."

Sasha pushed away from the table and watched Temple carefully. He wasn't above trying to drive a wedge between her and Kane. His mission, as far as he saw it, was to recover the chip and bring in the man who'd betrayed him. "What are you saying?"

"That Kane and I tracked the men who nabbed Anna to the club. Larry Tanner was the man who drove the car. He hangs out in one of the VIP rooms."

"Why are you telling me this now?" She didn't trust him but she didn't exactly not believe him either. Temple had always been a good friend to both her and Kane.

"Because I think that Kane may have double-crossed you the same as he did me."

She wasn't sure what to believe, but if Kane had double-crossed her, there wasn't anyplace big enough he could hide. She suspected he knew it. All of his actions had more the feeling of trying to get her out of the picture than actually betraying her. "I don't understand what's going on, Temple. Tell me everything."

He leaned across the table, a very intense look in his eyes. But it took more than that to intimidate her.

"If I come clean, will you?" he asked.

"Yes," Sasha said, but she knew that her compliance depended on what Temple had for her. Agencies typically didn't share information with each other because that information was worth its weight in gold. So if Temple had something that was worth the information they had gathered, she'd share. If not, she wouldn't. "You have a deal."

Temple took another sip of his coffee and then looked out the window. "I was working on a suspected terrorism case when I heard that Anna Sterling had been taken."

"With Kane?" she asked.

"Uh…no, Sasha. Kane's been suspended for the last two months."

"Why?" she asked. Shock and a quiet understanding started to splinter though her. Why hadn't he said anything to her? Kane was deeper in this than she'd suspected. Anna's kidnapping might just be the final straw as far as Kane was concerned.

What the hell was going on with him?

Temple just watched her. She realized he wasn't going to say any more on the subject. Mentally, Sasha was already going over the conversation she was going to have with Ano as soon as Temple left. Had her boss known that Kane was this far on the outside?

She suspected Ano did. Ano wouldn't accept a case like this without getting all the details. Something Sasha should have done instead of just charging off after her husband. But the fact that it was her husband had voided her information gathering. Her gut had screamed for her to save him. But she couldn't save someone who didn't want to be saved.

"If you don't want to tell me, you can leave. I'll go speak with your boss in the morning and get the entire story."

Temple stood and paced by the window. She wondered what he saw out there in the night. "It's not pretty. How much do you know about your husband's work?"

Not as much as she used to believe she did. And most of that was her fault because she'd closed up. She realized that Temple might know she worked for A.R.C. but he still had no comprehension that she was Nightshade. She hoped he never would know. "Enough."

"Vague. Nice answer, Sasha. You must be a pretty good agent." He gave her a half smile that made her want to smile back.

She realized that he was interrogating her. Playing the hard-ass and the nice guy. Waiting to see if either role had an effect on her. She'd done the same thing a time or two herself, so she just kept her expression cool. "I get by," she said. "Tell me about Kane. You can't shock me, Temple."

"We were working a white-slavery case. When it was over, two key players walked because of diplomatic immunity. Kane was pissed and didn't bother to keep everyone from knowing. The director wasn't too happy about it either. So together they took it all the way to the top."

"Why did Shubert suspend Kane?" Sasha asked. She knew what that was like. Could easily imagine Kane's anger at working hard to find out who was behind a scheme like that and then have his hands tied because diplomats played by different rules.

"He went to the embassy and made some direct threats to the men involved. They made a few calls and Kane was called on the carpet and told to lay off."

"And did he?" she asked, knowing the answer. Hell, she probably would have done the same thing. In fact, she had, a time or two. That was the main reason she worked for Renegade Company. They were multinational and at times had served justice instead of diplomacy.

"What do you think?" Temple glanced over his shoulder at Sasha, speaking in that wry tone of his.

"He didn't."

"That's right. He goes back and this time the director suspends him. Kane walked out." He'd turned back to the window and Sasha couldn't make out enough of his expression in the glass to be definite, but she thought she saw anger in Temple's eyes.

"And you didn't hear from him until the ransom note for Anna came to HMIA?" she asked after a few minutes had passed. She didn't want Temple to focus on all the reasons why Kane was on the outside. She might need Temple's help to bring him back in.

"We're friends, Sterling and I," Temple said, walking back to the table. He sat in the chair he'd vacated a few minutes ago, toying with his coffee cup. He stared into it as if it held the answers he was seeking. "I didn't abandon him. We met for drinks a couple of times. I was getting through to him. He was ready to come back to work."

"Then Anna was taken," Sasha said. It was the only thing that made sense. Kane was already tired of fighting with the Agency and with his superiors over his inability to get the justice he sought.

"Yeah. And Kane got the note and went totally bonkers."

"I thought HMIA got the note," Sasha said, sifting through everything that Kane had told her and what they'd pieced together themselves.

"No. Townsend sent it directly to Kane," Temple said.

Sasha shivered. Rubbing her arms, she closed her eyes and pictured the events differently. If Kane was sent the note…then, what had happened? "And Kane brought it to you?"

"Yes, we talked about it and started investigating, then something happened—I don't know what—but Kane walked into headquarters and walked out forty-five minutes later with the STAR list."

"Are you saying that Townsend never contacted HMIA and Shubert?" she asked, needing to be very sure of the facts at this point.

"Yes. Kane was the one he went directly to."

Sasha needed to think this through. Because the conclusions she was drawing didn't seem right. And she didn't want Temple to focus on them either. Because if she was right, then Kane was being targeted because he was a suspended agent. And Townsend knew enough about HMIA to realize that Kane could kiss goodbye any career plans he had of making his way up the ranks.

She took another sip of her coffee. But had a hard time swallowing it. Her stomach was swirling and she felt sick. "We didn't get that in our search for information. We did find a connection to von Buren and Townsend but its pretty weak."

"What is it?" he asked.

"Their sons both attended Eton. We haven't had a chance to determine if their connection is any closer. But I know from the playdates I've been on with Dylan that it's easy to meet parents and that business relationships can be formed from those meetings."

"Interesting. What are your next moves?" he asked.

Get Temple out of the house. Search Kane's rooms and offices then contact Ano. "What are yours?"

"Are we really back to that?" he asked.

"Yes, I think we are."

"Very well then." Temple stood and headed toward the front of the house.

"Temple, be careful."

"You too, Sasha. I'm afraid you're trusting the wrong man."

She let him out of the house and reset the alarm, his last words to her dancing through her head like a carnival barker's. Making her wonder if she should risk everything she'd worked hard to achieve for a man who didn't trust her enough to tell the truth.

Sasha picked up her Blackberry cell phone and made a quick call to Ano's private number. The call was answered on the second ring.

"Ano."

"It's Nightshade."

"What's up?"

"I just learned that HMIA was never asked for the STAR list. Townsend went directly to Sterling."

"Who told you this?"

"Temple. Does this match what you've heard?"

"I couldn't find out why the list was taken. Shubert is playing this very close to his chest."

"I would too. He's got a rogue agent who is one of the most dangerous masterminds of our time and now a second man who could be planning to join ranks with him."

"Have you found any indications of that?" Ano asked.

"No. I'm just pissed off."

"I can tell. Want me to send Charity to take over?"

"No. It was personal before because of Kane, but now…he lied to me. I can't leave this unresolved."

"Husbands lie to their wives all the time."

"I know that, but usually other people aren't put into jeopardy because of it."

"What's your plan?"

"Search the town house and gather any information I can."

"I'll be joining your breakfast meeting with Charity and Justice."

"Affirmative. Has Justice found anything new?"

"Not yet. But Orly is running the same information between the two of them, I have no doubt we'll uncover whatever is there."

"Me too. Okay, I'll be in touch later."

"Are you sure about this, Nightshade?"

Was she sure? Hell, she didn't know. She'd stopped analyzing as soon as Temple had told her that Kane was lying and manipulating her to act in a way to cover his tracks. The answer came to her in a rush. She wasn't letting any man use her again. "Yes. I'm sure."

She hung up before Ano could say anything else. Quietly she packed up her clothes and put the suitcase at the foot of her bed. She gathered the tools she'd need to search Kane's home office. This was absolutely the last thing she'd expected to do in her own home. Yet she had no choice. Kane was keeping secrets. Dangerous secrets that had jeopardized not just himself but their family and friends.

Unlike the last time when she'd decided it was better for her marriage to leave his room undisturbed, nothing was going to stop her from finding out if he had hidden any secrets in the house. Nothing would stop her from achieving her objective. She planned to search his bedroom before leaving as well.

She couldn't afford to let any emotions sway her. It was funny that she'd always feared rage, thinking it was the most dangerous thing. But tonight she thought affection might be just as dangerous.

Her little black gear bag held a camera, computer devices and lock-pick tools. Since she was already in the house, she wouldn't need to break in anywhere. Hurrying back down the stairs, she realized she wanted to find something. Anything that would make capturing Kane easier.

Her husband—no. Rogue agent Sterling. If only it were that easy to keep the distinction. But it wasn't. And never had been. That's why marriage was probably her biggest mistake.

She used a penlight instead of turning on the lights. Since she'd escorted Temple out of the house and went up to the bedroom, anyone watching the house would assume she'd gone to bed. She entered the office and closed her eyes to block out the memories as she was assailed by the scent of his aftershave. Of course, they'd been in the room before they'd left for Café de Paris.

Using a UV screen draped over the monitor to prevent any light from being seen outside, she booted up his computer.

Opening his desk drawers she found pens, matchbooks and a picture of herself and Dylan in the top one. She paused for a moment, running her finger over her son's little face. The picture had been taken when Dylan was only a week old. He was so tiny there. She hadn't realized how much he'd grown in the last few months from baby to sturdy toddler.

She turned the photo over. Kane's bold handwriting had labeled the picture with the exact date and place. Their marriage had still been good then. Both of them still operating under the illusion that there were no problems between them.

Or that the problems that existed could be ignored. Damn, when had things gone so bad? Because, for Kane to be so far outside of the Agency, he had to believe there was no reason to come back. There was no way he could believe that they could ever have a life together once he returned. Was that his plan? To save Anna at whatever the personal cost? Even his marriage? Even his life?

Slowly Sasha sank back in the chair, trying to find a way to still believe in Kane.

The computer beeped and made its melodic system up-and-running sound. Sasha closed the desk drawer and started searching for files that might have some bearing on this case. But she wasn't a computer expert. She pulled a thumb-size memory device from her black bag and copied the contents of the hard drive onto it. She'd give this information to Orly.

While saving the hard drive, she opened the other drawers in the desk. The bottom one was crammed with file folders that were labeled for bills. The second drawer was locked.

The top one held Kane's stationery. She pulled the paper out and found a folded sheet underneath the pile.

She opened the paper, finding a list of names.

Sasha
Temple
Townsend
Shubert
Ano
Malone

There was a question mark next to her name and Temple's. He'd underlined Shubert's name three times and Ano and Malone had big Xs next to them. She wasn't sure what that meant. None of the scenarios that flashed through her mind were reassuring.

Sasha laid the paper flat and took a quick photo of it before putting it back in the drawer. She knew the time for analysis wasn't in the middle of a search. But she couldn't help it. What was he trying to figure out? Allies, enemies?

It made no sense. She knew the connection between Shubert and Townsend, but was there a link she was missing between Ano, her dad and the one-time HMIA partners? She made a mental note to call her dad when she finished in Kane's office.

She retrieved her lock-pick tools and used them to open the second drawer. Inside was a steel-reinforced box that was also locked. Sasha pulled the box out and set it in the middle of Kane's desk. She held the penlight in her mouth and focused the beam on the lock box.

She started on the lock when the house alarm

beeped to show that a door had been opened. Sasha dropped the box back in the drawer and crept to the entrance of the study. She pulled her gun from the holster at the small of her back, counting to ten.

The alarm didn't go off. Whoever had entered knew the code or knew how to bypass it. She eased the door open and moved cautiously out into the hallway, ready to confront whoever waited there.

Chapter 10

Put your sword back into its place; for all those
who take the sword will perish by the sword.
                                                      —Matthew 26:52

Sasha eased her way down the hall, waiting in the
shadows until the intruder approached. Her pulse
rate slowed and everything seemed to move in slow
motion; her father called this the warrior instinct.

The intruder moved cautiously, careful not to
make any sounds. But there was no hesitation. He
knew where he was going.

It wasn't Kane. For one thing, the man was shorter
than her husband and a lot stockier. She spared a
thought for Omar, hoping he stayed upstairs and out
of the way.

As the man moved past her position, Sasha realized this was the second man they'd seen on the docks with von Buren. Was Kane already in league with Townsend's men? Sasha holstered her gun, knowing that she wanted answers from this man. The way her luck ran, if she shot him, she'd kill him, and then she'd find out nothing.

Deliberately she scraped her shoe on the floorboard. The intruder turned toward her, swinging with his right hand at her jaw. She blocked his punch with her left hand and brought her elbow up into his neck.

She grabbed his wrist with both of her hands. She rotated his wrists until his palm was facing upward, then secured her thumbs on the back of his hands, keeping her fingers securely wrapped around his lower hand and wrist. Maintaining the momentum, she pushed the hand downward, forcing him to submit until he was lowered to the floor.

He grunted and tried to strike out with his free hand, but Sasha brought the heel of her shoe down on the fleshy part of his free hand, using all her weight to force his hand to the floor.

She brought her left leg forward over his right arm and turned her body, applying pressure on the elbow joint. He groaned in pain. While Sasha held him captive, she searched for something to bind his hands, and found the zip cord she'd shoved into her pocket earlier. She bound his hands and forced him to his feet.

She pulled him out of the hallway and into Kane's office. Carefully she forced him into an armchair;

pulling the Glock from the holster she held the gun on him. Her hands didn't shake or waver. A bead of sweat appeared on his forehead and rolled slowly down the side of his face.

"Who the hell are you?" he asked, his voice rusty. Probably from the pressure she'd applied to his neck. If he cooperated and answered her questions, she'd offer him a glass of water before she hauled his ass down to the police station for breaking and entering.

"The lady of the house," Sasha said. She tried to make her breath even, using a technique she practiced in yoga. But adrenaline burned through her body and she shook with it.

His eyes narrowed and his creepy gaze moved over her body. "*You're* Sterling's wife?"

"Who were you expecting?" she asked. Not the question she wanted answers to. Who was this guy? And was this an inside job?

"The butler," he said with no touch of mockery in his voice. He glanced to the open doorway behind her. Sasha didn't turn to see if anyone was there, realizing that was just the opening the guy would need to move out of the chair. Damn, she needed backup.

"Was he expecting you?" Nightshade asked. She moved backward until she reached the study doors and locked them from the inside. She'd never considered that Omar might be working with Kane.

One thought really bothered her. Had Kane sent this guy? Did her husband care so little for her that he'd send a criminal into their home while she was there?

"No. But I was told he was the only one in residence."

"By whom?" she asked.

"Wouldn't you like to know."

"Yes, I would. And you're going to tell me. Who are you?"

"The bloody prime minister."

Sasha shook her head. Men never really took her seriously in this part of her job. One guy had even said she was just too girl-next-door-nice to be very intimidating. "Just because I'm a lady doesn't mean I can't get answers from you the hard way."

"You're welcome to try."

She smacked him hard across the face with her open palm. His head snapped back but he only glared at her. She drew back and struck him once more, deliberately hitting his nose hard enough to make it bleed but not break.

She didn't know if she could do it. Beat a confession out of someone. Only one other time had she been tempted and then she'd been in a full rage. The smell of her sister's blood had lingered in her nostrils and need for revenge had swamped her. Tonight she didn't want that madness. She desperately needed to keep a grip on her sanity. But she needed answers.

"Who are you?" she asked again.

He hesitated. He smirked at her in a way that made the hairs on the back of her neck stand up. She drew back her arm. "Tanner."

"Who do you work for?"

"I'm independent," he said. He shrugged his shoulders as far as the cuffs would allow and wiped his nose on his shirt. The blood would stain.

"Who sent you here?" she asked. If it was Townsend, Kane was in way over his head. If it was von Buren, they had the answer they'd been looking for about his involvement. What if Tanner had been sent by an interested third party?

Anyone in the global intelligence community had a vested interest in retrieving that list.

He stared at her and she didn't hesitate, this time letting the flat of her hand connect once again with his cheek. He groaned again.

"My boss."

"His name?"

"I don't know."

Sasha raised her hand and he flinched. Clearly, Tanner had had enough. Thank God.

"He calls on my mobile and gives me directions. If I do the job right, the money shows up in my account."

"What were you looking for tonight?" she asked. She figured Kane had the list with him. If Sasha couldn't find it, neither would the hired muscle.

"Sterling's family."

Fear lanced through her. She grabbed Tanner by the neck, forcing his head back, holding the gun under his chin.

"What were your orders?" she asked.

"Nab the wife and kid."

Kid. Townsend knew about Dylan. She wanted to grab her mobile and call her dad and verify that

Dylan was safe. But she didn't. She didn't even flinch when he'd said the words. She knew how to be cool.

At least on the outside. Inside she was seething. And the rage she'd battled for so long bubbled up inside her and she shook with it. Oh, God, not now. She couldn't give in. Couldn't let it take over. *Not yet.*

"How did you find out about them?"

"The boss knows everything."

"Yes, but *who* is your boss?"

"Lady, how the hell would I know? I just do the jobs. I don't ask questions."

"You've never seen the man?"

He glanced away from Sasha, down and to his left. Many experts agreed that looking away to the left meant that the suspect was lying. Sasha didn't know for certain. She'd hit Tanner from the right each time. He could just be resting that way.

"No."

Lying or not, she couldn't tell, and didn't think she'd get any more information from him on her own. Sasha stepped back from Tanner and grabbed the phone on the desk. She dialed A.R.C. headquarters and asked for backup.

Three hours later Sasha climbed into bed, exhausted. She wore her favorite silk long johns and a pair of socks she'd snagged from Kane's dresser. Where was Kane? For the third time she dialed his two-way pager and entered the simple message *Call me. S.*

So far he hadn't. She suspected he wouldn't. She closed her eyes but kept seeing Tanner's face and the chilling look in his eyes when he'd told her he was in London to nab Sterling's wife and kid. Two ARC operatives had arrived and taken Tanner away.

Getting out of bed, she walked through the connecting door that led to Dylan's bedroom. The crib was neatly made. The Noah's ark comforter and slew of plush animals filled it. She missed her son. Her arms ached to hold him. To reassure herself with his physical presence. Sighing, she picked up the cordless phone she was carrying.

She dialed her home number in Leeds. Her father answered on the first ring. "Dammit, girl. I told you, we're fine."

"Sorry, Dad. It's just…" How could she explain what she really didn't understand? She only knew that when more than five minutes passed she was overwhelmed with a feeling of panic that her son might have fallen into Townsend's clutches.

The sergeant major sighed. It was a deep, heartfelt one. For the second time in her life she was standing in her father's shoes. They were equals in this moment—both parents. Both unable to control the fate of their child and both damn pissed and scared about it.

"This is only the beginning, kiddo. Wait until he gets to be a teenager."

She thought of Jane Sterling, probably pacing the floor and unable to sleep because her daughter was missing. Sasha had spoken to her mother-in-law twice and still hadn't found the words to reassure her. Suddenly she realized there weren't any words. And she knew with a mother's insight that Jane would probably never be able to sleep or relax while Anna was out of her sight, when she was finally returned to Jane. She'd called earlier to warn her dad about the threat to Dylan, but this call was to soothe her own anxiety about her son.

"God, Dad, how do parents survive this worry?" she asked, unsure she'd be able to do it. She'd tried to manage her own weaknesses by keeping Kane outside of her heart and letting Dylan in. But had she made a tactical error? She knew her father loved her, but he'd always warned Sasha that letting her emotions sway her would be her downfall. And then when Caroline had been in trouble—real trouble— her emotions had let her down.

Charity always said that a woman's true strength came from her ability to care, but Sasha had grown up in a different environment and she'd never really been able to trust her own woman's strength. The one time she had…she didn't want to go there tonight.

"I think the love balances it out," her father said at last.

She closed her eyes. Tears burning at the back of them. Realizing in that moment how much she loved her dad and how thankful she was that he was exactly the man he was. "Thanks, Dad."

"Call back if you have to," he said before he hung up. She pictured her dad patrolling the house in Leeds. Keeping a vigilant watch over his sleeping grandson.

She closed her eyes again. This time, instead of

focusing on the threat, she forced herself to focus on the investigation. What did she know? Someone—probably Townsend—had hired Tanner to get more leverage against Kane. In a weird way, she was re-assured that Kane still hadn't surrendered the list.

It also meant that Townsend didn't believe Anna, as a hostage, had enough influence over Kane. Or, Sasha thought grimly, *Anna could be dead.*

Her heart clenched at the thought of the fourteen-year-old no longer alive. She wouldn't let herself dwell on that thought. She needed to focus on getting Anna back. So far, Sasha wasn't sure what she'd say when she talked to Jane. Kane hadn't mentioned his mother, but she knew that Kane wouldn't. He was even worse about emotional discussions than she was.

And he'd always borne the burden of being the head of the family. Mitchell Sterling had been killed in a terrorist bombing in the late 1980s when Kane was at Eton. In a moment of real honesty just before they'd gotten married, Kane had confessed that he'd gone into covert ops to in some way gain justice for his father's death.

She closed her eyes, remembering how raw he'd seemed. It was exactly what she'd felt later when Caroline was killed. Exactly what she'd never learned to control. But Dylan had added to her per-spective. It was as if a new life had given her the seeds to come to terms with the past.

She rubbed her arms and rolled over in bed, star-ing at the empty pillow next to hers. She was so tired of sleeping alone. The first few months after Dylan was born she hadn't been interested in sex but she was now. She needed that closeness with her husband. Needed to reassure herself that she was still womanly and not just momlike. Needed to reassure Kane that there was still a bond between them worth keeping.

This was getting her nowhere. Sitting up, she flicked on the nightstand light and pulled out a pen and paper. The truth was, she thought better when she could write the facts down. She debated going downstairs for a cup of tea but decided not to.

She made three columns on the pad, labeling each one Kane, Townsend and Nightshade. Under Kane she put the stuff she knew. He was being blackmailed to bring the STAR list to Townsend. Townsend had Anna, wanted the kid and wife. Why? She had a couple of theories and none of them put her at ease.

Under Townsend she wrote down STAR list, von Buren, Tanner and Kane. What did all these players have in common? Nothing on the surface. Kane had the STAR list, Townsend wanted it. Von Buren and Tanner had been seen together. Tanner did odd jobs for a "boss," probably Townsend. Von Buren's son and Townsend's son had been in school together.

She needed more information on the sons.

Her pager beeped and she glanced down at the display window. *Are you alone?*

The number was scrambled but she knew it was from Kane. Was he finally coming home? Did she want him too? She was still angry with him. But for the first time since Tanner had been taken away, some of the numbness left her. She put her pen and paper down on the table.

Yes.

Alone and cold and scared, she thought. Always after a fight or altercation she felt this wave of fatigue and fright. Never during the time when she was working, but afterward. No matter how many cups of tea she drank she still felt a chill that started deep in her bones.

But Kane was out there and she knew that he was thinking of coming home. Home to her? It had been a long time since either of them had been home to each other.

Sasha wasn't sure they'd ever really come to a place where they both felt as if they were home. She always felt that way when she held Dylan. She hoped Kane did too, but she didn't know anymore and was too tired to guess.

When he showed up she wasn't going to let him leave until he'd told her the truth…the whole truth this time and not the half bits she'd been accepting. She'd been patient with Kane but that wasn't happening any longer. They either worked together as a team or he could sit in a prison cell until she and her buddies from A.R.C. brought Townsend to justice.

She waited but no further message came. She climbed out of bed and crossed to the doorway that led to Kane's room. She opened the heavy wooden door. The bed held memories that she didn't really want to revisit tonight. The first time he'd made love to her had been in that big four-poster with the moon-light pouring in through the open window.

She wasn't giving in to her fears anymore. She was facing them. She entered the dark room and deliberately walked to the bed. Then sat right in the middle of it.

There had been a time they'd been happy…

Their wedding picture hung on the wall next to a framed picture of Kane's parents. Sasha looked at herself and felt the memories she'd locked away start to slide in. She closed her eyes but that only intensified them.

She remembered the feeling of that heavy white satin dress. Through the gauzelike veil she'd watched her father, with his eyes misty for the first time ever. He'd hugged her close, smelling of his cigars and that pine-scented aftershave he'd always worn.

"You sure about this guy?" he'd asked.

"Yes, Dad. I don't think there's another man out there who loves me enough to let me be me."

"If you ever change your mind…"

"What? You'll take care of him? No need for divorce."

Her dad laughed in that big booming way of his and she felt so safe. She'd forgotten what it was like to feel this way. God, she'd really missed this feeling. Maybe being on leave wasn't such a bad idea. She didn't have to look over her shoulder or scout the church for killers or terrorists or plant bombs.

All she had to do was walk down the aisle to Kane

Sterling. The man who'd talked her into starting a family with him. The man who'd promised her that they'd have the kind of life that poets wrote sonnets about. They'd be a modern-day Percy Blakney and his Marguerite. Two smart, social people who worked to make the world a better place.

Her hands started to shake when she heard the herald trumpets play the beginning chords of the wedding march. What if she was making the biggest mistake of her life?

Her father tucked her hand into the crook of his arm and they moved into position. Her two bridesmaids, Anna and Lydia, were already at the altar waiting. Charity was at the front as well and everyone in the church stood to face her.

Her stomach hurt so badly. She wanted her gun. Give her a Glock and a bad guy and she knew what to do. Give her a church full of people and a social situation where she was the center of attention and…she couldn't do it. Panic rose up in her and she turned away. But her father's firm grip kept her in place.

"I thought you were sure about this guy."

Her father's words pushed the panic away. This wasn't about a church full of people. This was about Kane and the promises they'd made to each other.

"Wait a second, Dad." Sasha pulled free of her father and lifted the veil so that she could see the groom better. There was Kane waiting for her at the front of the church. He looked as scared as she did. Strangely, knowing he wasn't confident reassured her as nothing else could.

She walked down the aisle on her dad's arm, and when Kane took her hand in his, she felt the warmth and strength in him. He quirked one eyebrow at her.

"What?" she asked under her breath.

"Wish we'd run off to Vegas instead of letting my mom have her way?"

She couldn't help the laugh that bubbled up. Leaning up, she kissed him hard and quick. "No way would I have missed seeing you sweat it up here."

"Sasha?"

She shook her head and turned around. Kane was standing in the doorway to his bedroom watching her. God, how long had she been standing here just staring at the picture?

"What?" she asked, hating the husky sound to her voice. But those memories and their wedding day always choked her up. Everything was so perfect for one shining moment. Things had changed almost immediately after that.

"You okay?"

"Yes. I was just looking at our picture."

He left his spot and came toward her with that easy masculine grace of his. He stood behind her, his hands on her shoulders. She felt the rasp of each breath he took as he looked at the picture.

"God, we look so young there."

Sasha tilted her head to the side and saw them through his eyes. "We didn't know too much about relationships."

"I can tell from your tone that you think we still don't."

"Well…"

"Woman, we just have to figure ourselves out first," he said. She wondered what he meant. She'd always felt as if she knew herself well. But Kane's words made her realize that she really didn't.

Chapter 11

A friend is like gold. Trouble is like fire.
Pure gold delights in the fire.
                                    —Jalil al-Din Rumi

Kane entered the room silently. He came in through her bedroom and paused in the doorway. The light from her room painted him in shadows. He stood there for a moment and she was very afraid that she'd lost him. That she'd never again see Kane standing in the light.

"I wasn't sure what kind of reception to expect," he said quietly. He held his left side a little stiffly. She noticed his MK23 was in his right hand. Kane was ambidextrous when it came to weapons.

"I'm not sure what kind you are going to get," she said after a few minutes. Anxiety and exasperation warred inside her. She'd been off balance since her father stepped out of the night with his disturbing news about Kane and everything that happened since then seemed to be shoving her further down the rabbit hole. Every time she caught her balance something else sprung out at her.

He took a half step into the room and now he was covered in the dark shadows. Nothing of his expression visible. Only the glint of light off the steel barrel of his weapon. "I shouldn't take as a good sign that you're in my bed?"

She forced herself to her feet. Not wanting to let him have any advantage. There was something sexually exciting about being here with Kane. This Kane who was in that nebulous region of maybe her enemy—maybe her ally. "I'm feeling kind of hostile."

"Me too."

"What the hell happened to you tonight?" she asked, hoping that the time for games was over.

He shook his head and walked into the room. He went to the nightstand and turned on the light. A mottled bruise covered his right cheek and his shirt was torn and splattered with blood. "You don't want to know."

Her gut screamed at her to clean him up, to mother him and make sure he was okay. But Kane had made it clear from the very beginning that he wanted a wife who didn't cling and didn't fuss over him. Sasha had never wanted to do that for any other man. But Kane always brought out the feminine instincts she didn't trust.

"I wouldn't have asked if I didn't."

"Sure you would have. Whatever role you play, Sasha, you're always thorough."

"And you're not? We have similar training," she reminded him. She'd once thought they had too much in common, but lately she'd started thinking that maybe they were different sides of the same coin. She was dwelling solely inside the law, he had been taking justice into his own hands.

"That's one of the reasons I'm not coming too close to you, Sasha."

"I'm not sure I follow."

"I'd want to kick your ass if you pulled something like I did." His words reassured her that he wasn't as far gone as she'd feared. Deep inside this stranger was the man she'd first fallen in love with.

"I do," she said, knowing it was true. "But I don't have the luxury of just indulging in my own anger. One of us has to think about the family we started."

He cursed sibilantly under his breath. "I'm trying to protect you, woman."

She crossed to him. She hated it when he did his macho thing. But she understood it. Kane could be very primitive man beating his chest dragging home fresh game to be prepared. But it didn't mean that she liked it. "Since when have I needed protecting?"

He turned away from her and went into the bathroom, turning on the light. "Hell, you never have. Do you have any idea how that makes a man feel?"

Kane went to the cupboard and took out a fluffy navy-blue towel monogrammed with his initials. He turned on the tap water and wet the cloth. Sasha stood in the doorway watching him for a minute before she went to him.

Taking the cloth from him, she dampened it and starting cleaning the blood from his face. "Like he's got a partner."

This close she saw the iris of Kane's eyes, watched them expand when she touched the side of his neck. Not for any reason other than to feel his warmth. His pulse increased and his nostrils flared.

"A partner? Is that really how you see us?" he asked, his hands resting at her waist. His long lean fingers stroked up under her shirt, rubbing a blind tattoo against her skin.

"I want to, Kane. But I have to be honest. I don't trust you. I suspect you don't trust me," she said. Shivers radiated from his touch, spreading through her body. Still susceptible to his touch, she thought, wishing for once that she wasn't.

"Why do you suspect that?" he asked silkily. He leaned closer, brushing his lips against her ear.

She dropped the washcloth. Framing his face in both of her hands, she stared into his eyes. She saw nothing there except his own fatigue and something deeper that she couldn't identify. She rubbed her lips gently over his. Loving the sweet peppermint taste of his breath. When he angled his head to take control of the kiss, she pulled back.

His hands moved up her back and he pulled her

into his arms, tucking her head against his shoulder. "Don't ask me any more questions. Just trust me."

She closed her eyes and breathed the scent of him deeply. But instead of reassuring her as it sometimes did, tonight it frightened her because she knew that Kane was playing a game that he might lose. And because of that, she couldn't depend on him. She slipped her arms around his waist and squeezed him tightly to her. Holding him even though she knew that he'd already slipped from her grasp.

She stepped back and looked up at him. "I can't because you've been lying to me."

He scrubbed his hand over his face and then crossed his arms over his chest. "What lies have I told?" he asked.

"I don't know where to start."

"The beginning?"

"Very funny."

"I find none of this amusing."

She couldn't say anything. "First of all, I think you should know that a man named Tanner broke in here tonight. His objective was to nab your wife and kid."

"Fuck."

"Precisely. I stopped him and he's in A.R.C.'s custody now."

"Is Dylan safe?"

"Yes. I called."

Kane reached for his mobile and Sasha listened to his side of the conversation. Hearing him speak to her dad and ask about their son. She was oddly reassured about Kane's involvement in Dylan's life and she took it to heart. Whatever happened between the two of them, he'd always be there for Dylan and she knew that was important.

Because every son needed to know his father. Kane hung up, looking ten years older than he had just five minutes earlier.

"Bloody hell, this is a mess."

"Maybe you'd better tell me what's going on."

"How much do you know?"

"Just what Temple told me."

He rolled his shoulders. "Let me get a shower and then we can talk…unless you want to join me?"

Sasha watched as Kane undressed, knowing she should leave but unable to do so. He turned on the water and slowly steam filled the room.

"This is one place where there's always been honesty between us," he murmured.

His chest was muscled, with a light dusting of hair that tapered down his stomach. Her fingers tingled to touch him. Decision made, she wasn't leaving him. Not now. She knew this settled nothing. Knew they were both still on the opposite side of an issue that was too big. Knew that she needed him tonight and sensed that maybe he needed her too.

"I still want answers," she said.

"Now?" he asked with a wicked grin on his face. His eyes skimmed down her firm body and she posed for a minute, fully aware of his reactions to her body. Feminine power rippled through her and she let him look his fill. Skimming her gaze over his body, she saw his reaction to her form, her curves, her womanhood.

She walked toward him. "What do you think?"

"That I'd tell you anything you wanted to hear in order to touch you," he said. There was a truth in his eyes that humbled her.

She felt the same way but she wasn't about to admit it. Kane had always held some sort of lethally dangerous power over her when they were alone like this.

"I don't want this to be part of the job," she said, but she wanted him so badly she knew she couldn't leave without making love to him.

"It never has been."

There was an honesty in him and in his reaction to her, his erection boldly jutting against the inseam of his pants. Tilting her head toward him, she lifted her hands to the bottom of her shirt and slowly opened one button and another until her stomach and belly button were revealed.

"God, woman, get over here."

She shook her head. He wanted her. There was a power in that she couldn't deny enjoying. "You come to me."

He did, walking to her until their chests brushed. The hair on his abraded her nipples, making them tighten. He skimmed his hands down her torso. Head bent, he watched her body's reaction to his. The calluses on his palms stimulated her, shivers spread throughout her body from his warm touch.

She scraped her nails down his chest, teasing his

nipples. He moaned her name. He closed his eyes, his head falling back. She leaned up on tiptoe and tongued her way down his neck, stopping at the base to suckle gently at his pulse point. His erection leaped between them. His hips jolted forward, searching for the notch in her thighs and nestling there.

She widened her legs to accommodate him. He felt so good there. His hands moved both of them, encompassing the globes of her breasts. She felt full and shifted in his embrace, trying to make him hurry, but Kane was a patient lover.

Tonight, though, Sasha needed mind-numbing sex. Not sweet soul-searching lovemaking. She needed to forget and she couldn't if he made love to her this way. She reached between their bodies and worked his zipper down, pushing his jeans and underwear down his legs. He was full and hard.

She reached between his legs and cupped his sac. He moaned her name. She scored him lightly with her fingernails and felt his balls draw up against his body and then he expanded, growing fuller and more engorged. She stroked him a few times, ending each stroke by running her finger across the tip of him. The third time she did it, she felt a drop of wetness at his tip.

"Eager?"

"You have no idea," he said. He smoothed his hands down her body, pushing her leggings down. "It's been too long."

He lifted her and carried her to the counter around the sink, setting her down roughly on its cold marble surface. He dropped to his knees, burying his face between her legs. "I've missed the scent of you."

He murmured the words against the inside of her thigh. He parted her silky curls and leaned even closer. He inhaled deeply and then opened his mouth, breathing over her aroused flesh. She jumped at the first touch of his tongue against her sensitive skin.

Tunneling her fingers through his hair, she held him to her. Draped her legs over his shoulders and watched him worship her body. Watched him taste her deeply until everything inside her started to tense and clench. She needed more. She felt so empty. She lifted her hips toward each caress of his tongue.

Kane thrust one finger into her sheath then added a second. Pushing upward inside her until he found her sweet spot. His tongue and fingers worked their magic until everything in her lower body clenched once, then twice, and she came.

Kane stood and thrust into her body that was still rocking with her orgasm. He pushed himself deep inside her then held still until the tremors stopped rocking through her.

Deliberately she tightened around him. She felt him grow even larger. He slid his hands to her breasts, scraping his nail over the tips of her nipples.

Reaching behind him, she cupped his buttocks in her hands, running her finger down the furrow between his cheeks. Kane loved that. He immediately started thrusting. She slid her hands lower, carefully running her nail between his legs and pressing on his perineum. He grunted and thrust harder.

He slipped his arms under her thighs, lifting her legs and opening her for deeper thrusts. The angle of his entry was perfect, each thrust hitting her deep inside where she needed it, and it was long before she felt the familiar rush to completion. Kane's breath huffed in her ear and she turned her head, seeking his mouth.

She caught his lips with hers. He bit at her lips, gently, and then thrust his tongue deeply inside. She was filled with him. Her mouth, her womanhood...her senses. Totally surrounded by Kane, she felt as if she'd found something that had been missing for so long.

His hips jerked more quickly between her legs and she clenched his buttocks tightly. Felt him stiffen and then come inside her. She closed her eyes and felt her own orgasm approaching. Kane continued thrusting until she clenched around him. Her head fell to his shoulder.

No words were said. She knew that despite what she'd wanted, they'd had soul-sex. Their souls needed that melding. She also knew that she wasn't going to let this man take any steps that would put him beyond reach. She needed him always.

He lifted her tenderly in his arms and carried her into the steaming shower. He soaped her body and rinsed her. She took the soap from him and did the same for him. Lingering over the bruising on his face. Wanting to ask how it had happened. But allowing him to silence her with a soft touch on her lips.

He washed her hair then she did the same for him. They both dried off quickly. And Kane lifted her in his arms again and carried her into his dimly lit bedroom. Pulling back the covers, he placed her in the center of the bed.

There was still so much to be said and she felt as if her job as an agent demanded she get some answers. But the other part of her—the wife—urged her to enjoy this time of peace with her husband because she knew how quickly it could all fade away.

"Kane—"

"Not now, Sasha. Let me hold you. Just for tonight."

She nodded. He turned off the lamp on the nightstand and climbed into bed beside her. Reaching out to pull her into his arms. He fitted the two of them together. She lifted her leg over his hip until they were locked as closely as they could get.

She ran her hands down his back, offering him the comfort he needed to drift asleep. But sleep evaded her because she knew that the decisions facing her were tougher than any she'd ever made. And the consequences for choosing poorly were higher than she wanted to pay.

Kane stirred when the alarm in Sasha's room went off. Reluctantly she lifted her head from his shoulder. A bit of gloomy daylight passed through the seam between the heavy curtains. She moved out of the bed and away from her husband. It had been a long time since he'd really felt like her man, but last night had reaffirmed everything.

She hurried into her room, turned off the alarm and started dressing for the day. She couldn't leave

Kane alone to go to her meetings for the day. It was time for a serious heart-to-heart.

She pulled on a matching silk bra and panty set in navy blue. Then sat on the bed. His scent lingered on her skin and in her mind. Complications she'd never faced before now added to her swirling thoughts about this case. So much to do, so little time to do it.

Flinging herself back on the comforter, she stared at the ceiling. Searching for answers to questions she didn't really want answered. But in the end she'd never really run from reality and she wouldn't this time. Kane had to come clean or she was taking him in.

Decision made, she crossed to her armoire, pulling out a pair of Calvin Klein faded jeans. She pulled them on and groped around for her thick black leather belt, looping it around her waist. She had her hand on a screen-printed T-shirt. "Wardrobe choices that tough this morning?"

She glanced over at Kane. He'd pulled on a pair of faded jeans and leaned against the doorjamb. He had stubble on his cheeks and a love bite on his neck. He looked as if he'd had a long hard night. She felt the same.

"No problems with the wardrobe…you, however, are a different matter."

He entered her room, hesitated for a moment, as though he was going to come to her. She crossed her arms over her stomach, knowing that despite her training she was first a woman and couldn't really be an agent and a wife at the same time.

Kane must have picked up on her tension. Instead of coming to her, he sat on the padded bench at the foot of her bed. Stretching his long legs out, he rested his hands on his bare stomach. "What will it take to ease your mind?"

Her mind unfortunately had taken a leave of absence. It seemed her vacation from sexual awareness was over. Flooded with images of last night, she had to close her eyes to refocus, regroup her thoughts. Anna Sterling—missing. Kane Sterling—rogue and liar.

She turned away from him and chose her shirt. A red-white-and-black spandex one with three-quarter sleeves that had a graphic image of the Eiffel Tower and the word Paris on it. "We have to talk."

He sighed, scrubbed a hand over his jaw. "I don't suppose you could just go home to Dylan and leave this to me?"

She shook her head. If she had been that kind of woman, Kane and she never would have gotten together. "Does that sound like something I'd do?"

"No, it doesn't. Sometimes I wish you *were* a different woman."

The words hurt. Of all the problems they had, she thought he at least accepted who she was. But she couldn't change, for him or any other person. "I'm sorry I can't be anyone else."

"I know. I don't think I'd love you if you were. But it would make life a lot easier."

To hear him speak of love this morning made her uneasy. He had to know she was contemplating arresting him and turning him over to A.R.C. or even

HMIA. He had to know it. And he was shoring up his position. Or was he?

"Tell me everything," she said, crossing to her nightstand and picking up her pad and paper. Deliberately, she moved away from Kane but it didn't really diminish his effect on her. She still tingled from last night. Her thighs were pleasantly sore and she wished the alarm hadn't gone off so they could've woken each other up.

"About?"

"Where did you disappear to last night?" she asked, jotting the question on her notepad. She had to be logical, and the only way to do that was to remember that Kane was a suspect.

He rubbed his eyes and looked away from her. When he looked back, the stranger she'd first seen on the docks in Southampton was back. "There was someone waiting for me in the VIP room."

"Townsend?" she asked.

"No, that bastard hasn't come close to me," he said.

That made sense. Townsend had to know a meeting with Kane wasn't going to be something he could control. And Townsend hadn't evaded capture for so many years by being stupid. "Man or woman?"

"A woman. I didn't get her name. She just gave me a message and a location."

Sasha jotted down the notes. "Where?"

"The Candy Box."

"Another club?"

"Yes, I went there, was directed to an alleyway.

There was a discussion with some men—I'm assuming they work for Townsend. When I wouldn't give them what they wanted, they tried to force me to tell them where I hid the list. I refused and came back home."

Simple words that hid she knew a very complex situation. Kane had taken a beating and the fact that he was here meant he'd given one back. "Are there any bodies that will have to be explained?"

"They were breathing when I left," Kane told her.

"Do we know for sure that Townsend is behind this?"

Kane nodded. "Yes, each note I've received has been from him."

"Why didn't you tell me that he sent the ransom notice directly to you?"

"Because then you'd ask some uncomfortable questions."

"Like, why is my husband suspended?" Sasha demanded.

"Exactly like that. And I was afraid you'd start putting two and two together."

Sasha couldn't argue with that. "And getting that Townsend thinks you're a weak link."

"Indeed."

"Is that the plan?" she asked.

"What plan? I'm suspended, remember?"

"Temple thinks you're crazy."

Kane pinned her with a haughty look. "I don't give a bloody damn what Temple thinks."

"I think you're crazy."

"Hell, woman, you should know better than that."

"Do you even have the STAR list?" she inquired at last.

"Yes."

"Am I part of your cover? Is A.R.C. working its ass off to make Townsend believe you really are on the outside?"

Kane said nothing. He stood and walked over to her. His hand was heavy on her shoulder and she stood stiff and still. "I can't tell you any more."

"If you don't, I'm taking you in."

"Sasha, don't do this."

"I'm not the one who has put us in this situation. You are."

He held her shoulders in his tight grasp. Leaning down, he kissed her hard and deep. The embrace was like their lives, full of anger, affection and tinged with a sadness that made her heart break in two. Because she was just coming to realize how much they needed each other to really be happy with their lives.

Chapter 12

The wise man in the storm prays to God, not for
safety from danger but for deliverance from fear.
                              —Ralph Waldo Emerson

Sasha pushed away from Kane and walked out of
the room. He wasn't going to give her any more answers. She was tired of asking and forcing him to tell
her things he didn't want to.

"Sasha, wait."

She paused and looked back at him but didn't turn
all the way around. There was hell in his eyes and it
echoed the feeling that swamped her. Who would've
thought that one brief affair that had seemed so perfect would have led to this?

"I…there's more going on here than I can tell you," he said.

She should have grabbed her gun earlier. She'd already figured that this town house was compromised, and it wouldn't take Townsend long to figure out that Kane's wife was the agent code-named Nightshade. The agent who'd almost brought him in. The agent who planned to put an end to his career on the other side of the law.

"Just give me enough to make a decision, Kane. I want to help you. But if you won't let me, then I'm going to do it my way."

"And to hell with the consequences?" he asked.

She wished she knew what he was thinking, but she'd never really been able to understand him. He'd proven that he wasn't above using their relationship to manipulate her and she wasn't going to let him do that again. "It's not my first choice."

"Fuck." He paced into his room and she stood where she was in the hallway, unsure what he was doing. He returned a moment later with a white oxford-style shirt on, unbuttoned. His leather jacket—also open. Shoes in one hand, socks in the other and his gun tucked into his waistband.

"Let's talk downstairs," he said, pushing past her to lead the way.

"Just a minute," she said, returning to her room and putting her Glock in the holster at the small of her back. She grabbed her notes, cell phone and two-way pager. She wasn't taking any more chances and letting Kane out of her sight. She could move with what she had. Honestly, she didn't need anything other than her gun.

"Traveling lightly?" he asked from the doorway. He was traveling the same way, so she didn't think he had any room to talk. They both knew that this was the crucial time in a case and they both were always ready to roll at a moment's notice.

Working together made her realize all the ways they were alike and all the ways he was so damn stubborn. He was a hardheaded man. If just once he'd listen to her, they'd probably not have any more arguments.

"Yes. I'm not going to be caught off guard again," she said, leading the way downstairs. She paused in the foyer, contemplated going into Kane's study, but she wanted to ask him a few more questions. She also wanted him to take her in there and show her what was in the locked box. If he didn't, she'd take him to Ano and come back for it herself.

"Let's talk in the breakfast room. I'll cook," he said. Kane wasn't a gourmet chef but he was better in the kitchen than she was. Especially with breakfast, which he considered to be the best meal in his bachelor repertoire.

"Where's Omar?" she asked, not having seen the butler around this morning. And there was no sign he'd been in the kitchen today. The coffeepot stood empty.

"I sent him to visit his family in the country," Kane said. He started gathering ingredients for breakfast.

"When?" she asked. As far as she knew, he hadn't

had time to speak to Omar. Had she slept through him getting out of bed last night?

"Before I joined you in my bedroom," he said. He took a frying pan from the pot rack and turned on the gas stove.

"Did you know that Tanner guy had come here before I told you?" she asked. He'd never really answered her questions last night.

He nodded. "Omar let me know."

"He's an agent?" More secrets. Did she really know anything about this man? She leaned against the counter and made more notes. Kane wasn't going to be operating alone for much longer.

"Totally freelance and only for me. He gathers information when I can't move freely into an area."

"Don't you think you should have told me that?"

"When did you need to know?" he asked, laying thick pieces of bacon in the frying pan. They sizzled and smelled delicious. Her stomach growled. She couldn't remember the last decent meal she'd eaten. Certainly it was before her dad had shown up in the middle of the night and rocked her nice safe suburban-mom world.

"There are too many secrets between us, Kane."

"I'm not the only one keeping them, am I?"

Sasha didn't want to talk about hers. Didn't want to face the fact that the problems in her marriage stemmed directly from the secrets she'd carefully guarded for too long. "Yours are the only ones causing us problems."

"Touché. Do you think you can sheath your claws long enough to eat bacon and eggs if I fix them?"

"Sure. I'll make the toast."

"No, *you won't*. I don't like it burnt."

Kane actually seemed in a lighter mood than he had since the beginning of this entire thing. "Suit yourself."

He made breakfast while she made notes and sent a message to Orly on the two-way pager. She asked him to come to the house instead of A.R.C. headquarters.

"This is nice," Kane said as he set plates on the table.

"Breakfast? I assume Omar makes one every day for you."

"Thanks, smart-ass, but I meant you and I together. The only thing missing is *D*."

It *was* nice actually. "Why don't we do this more often?"

"Because you're usually not interested."

Looking down at her plate, she refused to acknowledge the truth of what he said. It had been a long time since she'd really enjoyed her marriage and, clearly, Kane had felt that.

"It's not that I'm not interested."

"Then what is it?"

"I…it's hard to explain and we really have enough to deal with now. I'd like to hear more about what's going on between you and Townsend." She toyed with her fork. God, she'd never anticipated that Kane would go here—ever. She didn't want to talk about their marriage and the problems in it.

Sasha knew that she'd been responsible for her share. Once their honeymoon was over, Kane had immediately gone back to work and so had she.

She'd taken a case in the United States because it had involved her sister, Caroline, and she'd wanted to save her.

Kane had been deep undercover and Sasha had tried only once to contact him when she realized that Caroline and her son, Seth, had been taken. Then she'd done what she did best. Locked her emotions away and started functioning like a robo-cop. She and Charity had always joked that that's what they were. But in reality, Sasha knew she had a switch deep inside that she flipped when cases got too intense for her.

She still remembered the smell of that place. Caroline and Seth had been held in a dilapidated farmhouse thirty miles south of Lake Okeechobee in the middle of nowhere. The Florida air had been thick with the smell of rotting sugarcane. Sasha and Orly had driven into town dressed in jeans and checkered shirts. Their vehicle looked like a run-down pickup on the outside, but Orly had souped up the engine and that baby was just as finely tuned as a Mercedes.

Because of the area they were in, they'd had two rifles in the open on a gun rack mounted behind the driver's seat, as did most of the locals. It had taken them three days to find the house where Caroline was being held. She'd been beaten and starved. Seth was in little better condition.

When Sasha had entered the dirt-floored barn where they were being kept, Seth had been curled on his side with his head resting on his mother's lap.

Caroline had looked up with a feral expression that Sasha hadn't really understood in her soul before she'd had Dylan.

She'd relaxed marginally when she recognized Sasha. Caroline had been gagged, so the first thing Sasha did was remove it. "Can you walk?"

"I'll try. But they broke my leg when I tried to escape the first time."

Sasha nodded. The pain her sister must be enduring made a wild kind of rage well deep inside her. She'd always protected others and, for the first time, her own family was in danger and she felt almost powerless to help them.

"I'll take Seth back to my partner and come back for you."

"Do that. Make sure you get Seth to safety. Promise me, Sasha."

"I promise. I'll take care of him."

"I always wanted a sister," Caroline said. Her words made no sense for this time and place and Sasha wondered if her sister was hallucinating.

"Me too."

"But you had one. Dad's girlfriend's daughter."

"Not really. Not like you," Sasha said. Though she knew the words for a lie. She was close to Charity. Closer than she was to Caroline. Closer than she wanted to be to Caroline.

She bent and lifted Seth. He moaned and opened his eyes. "Mama…"

"Go with your aunt."

"No. I won't leave you," he said, starting to cry.

"Take him, Sasha. Keep my baby safe."

Sasha turned away from her sister and ran out of the barn in the direction of Orly. "Orly, I've got the boy. Meet me. Caroline's leg is broke…I'll have to go back for her."

"Gotcha. I'm en route."

She'd kept running, though carrying a six-year-old boy who was struggling to get back to his mother was difficult. The explosion that rocked the air made her pause, but she knew even before she turned around and saw the flames and smoke lighting the sky that Caroline was dead.

"Mama!"

Sasha held her nephew tighter in her arms and tried to ignore the fact that tears were running down her face. Oh, God. Don't let it be true, she thought. But in her hard realist heart she knew it was.

"What is it, Sasha?" Kane asked.

She rubbed her arm and glanced over at him. She'd completely forgotten that he was still in the room with her. "Nothing."

"I can't be your husband if you don't let me in."

"Trust me, Kane. This isn't something you want in on."

"Yes, it is. I want it all—good and bad. That's what gives a marriage strength."

She shook her head. She couldn't do it. Already she was reliving things she'd vowed to never remember. And her arms ached to hug her own son. To keep him safe and to never hear that anguished cry that had come from Seth's mouth. The only way she could do that was to finish this case as quickly as she could and get back to him.

Kane smoothed his fingers over hers and pulled her hand into his grip. He held her as if she was fragile, precious, something important to him. She swallowed around the uncomfortable feelings. "I'm not letting this go. If it weren't for worrying for Anna's safety, this would be what I dreamed of. You by my side, everything coming together. This is what I envisioned when I asked you to marry me, Sasha."

"I—"

"Don't," he said, covering her lips with his fingers. "No excuses. No half truths. Just know that I'm waiting here for you if this is the kind of marriage you want."

She took a deep breath. Her life had been building toward this confrontation for a long time. And it wasn't one with Kane but with herself. She had to decide if she was going to continue hiding in the country or if she was going to trust her gut and her instincts enough to actually come back to life.

There was a knock at the back door and Kane dropped her hands and pulled his gun. Sasha grabbed her gun as well, both of them sliding from the table in a familiar partnership.

Kane signaled that she should open the door. Sasha motioned she understood. Kane grabbed her wrist as she moved past him. Something in his eyes reassured her that she was close to getting the answers she needed from him. Answers that had eluded them both for too long.

She stepped up to the side of the door frame. It was easy to shoot someone through the door. Though she suspected Kane's house would have reinforced-steel doors, she wasn't taking any chances.

"Who is it?" Sasha asked, making her voice deep and commanding.

"Bloody hell, Sasha. It's Orly and I'm freezing my arse off out here."

She unlocked the door and opened it but didn't holster her gun, and neither did Kane. "Good morning to you two, too."

"Were you followed?" Sasha asked as he moved into the room and closed and relocked the door behind him. Orly dumped a large leather backpack on the floor and rubbed the back of his neck. His hair was still damp, she assumed from a shower. And without his usual spikes, he looked like a respectable kind of guy.

"You invited him?" Kane asked. He didn't sound too happy about it.

"Yes. Did you want to have to wait for backup when it's time to move?" Regardless of what happened with Kane, she knew the next twenty-four hours were going to be hopping and she wanted her team by her side. She'd hesitated to contact Charity because she wasn't sure yet what Kane knew and she didn't want to risk her friend going to Ano with the information.

"Who says I need backup?"

"I do."

"I hate to interrupt your love play but can I get a cup of coffee?"

"You know where the cups are," Kane snapped.

"I do. But you both still have your guns trained on me."

"Oh." Sasha put hers away and Kane did the same. He gave her one of those little half smiles of his as he did it.

"Sasha, make the man some toast," Kane said. He sank back into his chair at the table and started eating his breakfast.

"Hey, what'd I do to piss you off?" Orly asked Kane. He'd retrieved a coffee cup and was leaning back against the countertop.

"I told you to keep her in Leeds," Kane said.

Sasha stared at Kane. So much for her female instincts saying they were forging new ground. Now she knew how Alice had felt when she'd stumbled down that rabbit hole.

"Since when do you give Orly orders?" she asked. Orly shrugged at her and concentrated intensely on his coffee. Wondering what the hell she was to either man. Was this friendship and business that she and Orly had created all part of some strange ruse?

"Since I wasn't sure if my wife was ready to return to work," Kane said, pushing himself to his feet.

"By the way, I take orders from myself where you're concerned, Sasha. I owe you my life and I make my decisions accordingly," Orly said hurriedly.

"You think you know my wife better than I do?" Kane demanded.

"I see her more clearly because I don't love her the way you do."

"I'm standing right here," Sasha said irritably. Both men looked at her. "Is Anna even missing? Or was this all your idea to get me to go back to work? I thought you liked the small security business."

"I wish that's all it was, Sasha," Kane said. "But Anna is really missing. That bastard Townsend thinks I'm the key to taking down the cooperation between the global intelligence community and HMIA."

"Why does he think that?" she asked, glad to no longer be the topic of conversation. She tucked away all the emotions she felt about these two men who were all that remained of her old life. All that she'd let herself keep, and realized that the entire time she'd thought she was making a new life, they'd been waiting for her to come back to her old one.

Kane sat back down and gestured for Orly to take a seat at the table. "Because I'm out in the cold, just like he was."

"And how does he know that?" she asked. That had been bothering her. Townsend was very well informed for a man on the outside of the agency.

"Shubert thinks we've got a mole in HMIA," Kane said quietly. The confession wasn't an easy one for him to make. Especially because she and Orly worked for another organization.

"Any ideas who?" she asked after it was clear he wasn't going to continue on his own.

"No. It could be anyone. Even *Temple*. So I don't want you talking to him anymore."

She filed that away. Temple didn't seem like a double agent. He was too angry at Kane and the entire setup. But he had been at the house right before Tanner had arrived last night. He also knew that Sterling's wife was in London.

"Did you set up Anna?" she asked Kane, because it didn't fit with the man she thought he was.

"Never. Townsend is crafty, I'll give him that. He contacted me once when I was first suspended. I turned him down flat. Two weeks later, Shubert calls me into his office and we talked. Afterward, I stormed out. By the time I got home, Anna was gone."

"I think your plan backfired, am I right?"

He nodded. "Somehow, Townsend knew that we were planning something. Shubert refused to consider letting me take the STAR list even as a decoy."

"Do you have it?"

"Hell, yes. Something did snap inside me, Sasha. My baby sister is in the hands of one of the most elusive criminals of our time. My boss has egg on his face and I am still officially suspended."

"Do you have any idea where Anna is?"

He shook his head. "Townsend's message to me last night was to be in Paris in two days. If I brought the list and came alone, Anna would be waiting for me."

"We need a plan. Have you told me everything, Kane? I don't want any more surprises."

"That's it. But we don't need a plan. I'm going alone," Kane announced.

"Townsend will capture you and the list."

"Thanks for your faith in my abilities."

"Hey, you're a good agent but you're still only one

man. I'd like to bring Charity and Justice in on this," Sasha said.

"No."

"I'm sorry you feel that way, but this is my case and I'm in charge," Sasha insisted.

Kane cursed under his breath. "I can't. Listen, I'm not an actor. I'm mad, Sasha, and I don't care what happens to that list if I can't get my sister back. Do you understand what I'm saying?"

"Better than you know. Let's get a plan together. We can outwit Townsend. He's too used to winning and expecting us to follow agency protocol."

Kane didn't exactly agree but he leaned back in the chair. She still saw hell in his eyes and she knew that he blamed himself for Anna being taken. Because he'd agreed to let himself be bait and left his entire family vulnerable.

"Is someone watching this house? Or do you really believe that Temple is the mole?" Sasha asked. She couldn't believe that her child's godfather was acting against Kane, but at the same time she could.

Kane paced to the window. She sensed he wanted to stare out, but instead he stood to the side, well out of sniper range. A weak bit of sunlight pooled on the floor at his feet. "I don't know. I'm not willing to take the risk of trusting him without proof."

Sasha closed her eyes and focused inward. Her dad always said the best plans were the ones that were kept simple. Two things stood out in her mind. One—whatever Bruce knew, he was clearly angry with Kane. Two—he'd be susceptible for them to use. "I suggest we use Temple to get information to Townsend."

"What if he's not the mole?"

"He's clearly still reporting in at work. He's been assigned to find you and bring you in. So, if it's not Temple, then it's his boss or someone in his chain of command."

"That fits Townsend's profile. His resentment of the Agency goes back to his days of being partners with Shubert. The first note I got from him intimated that I wouldn't have been suspended if Temple hadn't been sabotaging my career."

"Do you believe that?" Sasha asked.

"No. I've always trusted Bruce. But that doesn't mean he couldn't be set up without his knowing it. You're both familiar with how orders are sometimes. You only know your part of the operation."

"Whatever the case may be, we'll count Temple as part of the enemy camp until he's proved otherwise," Sasha said. "I'll cut contact with A.R.C. and you and I can leave for France in a couple of hours. I'll let Temple know that I'm on the outside and I've joined with you."

"I still like my plan better," Kane said. He wasn't much of a team player. He'd worked with Temple for more than fifteen years but even then he did these kind of rogue things a lot.

The time for Kane being in charge was over. When she'd walked that lonely path, she'd made mistakes. Mistakes she was still trying to cope with. Without revealing her own weaknesses to Kane, she hoped to keep him from making the same errors she had. "Forget it. You're not the Lone Ranger anymore. You've got Orly and me at your back. Can you give the microchip with the STAR list on it to Orly?"

"Why does Orly need it? I'm not turning it over to A.R.C."

"I'm not asking you to. I want him to create a new list that mirrors the original but that also has a virus that will shut down Townsend's computer network."

Kane didn't respond right away. He paced the floor in what she knew was his processing mode. He was one of the savviest agents she'd ever met, and working with him felt right. This was where they could become a really successful couple. But she was still afraid to risk it.

"Townsend will be suspecting that," Kane said. "He's not your usual type of criminal, Nightshade. He knows all our procedures."

"Orly's the best at what he does," Sasha said, turning to her partner. "Can you do it so that Townsend won't notice?"

"Probably," Orly told her. "I'd have a better chance of doing it with Justice at my side. That woman is pure magic with computers." Orly was already making notes on his handheld laptop. The computer was light, thin and no bigger than a paperback book.

Sasha glanced at Kane. The more people who knew the plan, the greater chance of being exposed. But Townsend would believe that HMIA wouldn't want to air their dirty laundry to any other intelligence agency. He was banking on the fact that Kane and Shubert wouldn't trust anyone else.

"Ah, hell," Kane said, rubbing the back of his neck. "Call her in."

"Let me go to her," Orly said. "We don't believe in coincidences, which means the house is being watched. I didn't really take any precautions against being seen."

She hadn't asked him to. She'd just wanted someone else here in case she had to take Kane in. Was she really going to do this? Turn her back on the Company once again? Because she knew that Ano wouldn't approve of this operation unless she was brought in. Field agents had some leeway in making decisions but it always came back to Ano for campaigns of this magnitude.

"Sounds good," she said to Orly. "Kane and I will pack up. Are we driving to France or taking other transportation?"

"Driving. I want my own wheels," Kane said. He had a sleek black sports car that he'd gotten from HMIA that was outfitted similarly to Orly's Land Rover. It was a sexy command vehicle that was all Sterling needed when he was working.

"I'll be in contact, Orly," Sasha said. "We need the microchip in Paris tomorrow night at the latest."

"I'm not giving Orly the chip," Kane said.

Sasha wanted to kick him. He was so frustrating. It seemed as if every step they took forward, Kane then pulled them farther back. "Why not?"

"Because, Nightshade, it's the only bargaining power I have at this moment."

The hell of it was she understood where he was coming from. But she needed him to really commit to her. The list would go a long way to assuage her doubts that this wasn't the right move. "You can trust us, Sterling."

Kane said nothing else. She recognized the stubborn look in his eyes. It was the same one Dylan used when he wanted to keep his pacifier after he got out of bed. Thinking of Kane as a surly toddler didn't re-assure her. He was being unreasonable and there was something in his stance that said he knew it.

Orly just watched the tableau like the spectator he was. Embarrassed to be having a stare-down with her husband, Sasha turned away from him. "Stalemate?"

"We have a copy of the list we can use to create a dummy. But I need to know how HMIA front-loads their data. Are you willing to let me look at that?" Orly said, offering a solution that would keep the peace.

"Yes," Kane said. "When you join us in France, I'll give it to you then."

"I'm out of here. I'll be in contact with Sasha."

Orly left and Kane bolted the door after him. Then he sat at the table and she realized he wasn't going to acknowledge the fact that he still didn't trust her.

"Would you go to Ano before leaving?" he asked.

"No," Sasha said. "I'd just disappear. Why would I tell Temple?"

"You wouldn't unless he found you. What did you tell him last night?"

"Nothing."

"What did he say?"

Sasha didn't know if she could tell him. She'd thought about Bruce's words, really thought about them. The fact that she had addled her. She'd always believed the best of Kane, but lately…

"Sasha, what did he say?"

"That I had trusted the wrong man."

"Do you believe him?" he asked.

Sasha didn't want to lie and wasn't sure what the truth was at this moment. Instead, she walked away from Kane.

Chapter 13

No coward soul is mine.

—Emily Brontë

Alone in her room, she packed her valise, putting a picture of Dylan on the top of the bag before she zipped it closed. Kane was next door in his room. They hadn't always had separate rooms. But the last time they were in London she'd been in her queen-bitch role and Kane had ticked her off.

She'd spent the next six weeks redoing this room that used to be an upstairs study. Her study actually. Kane had suggested she use this room to work out of because he knew she got restless at night and she'd want to be close to Dylan.

Her cell phone rang. She checked the caller-ID

screen and saw that it was scrambled. It was probably Orly. She'd been expecting his call since he left. "Sterling."

"It's Dad."

"Hey. I was getting ready to call you."

"Tell me about it later. Listen, Dylan's not looking too good."

"Does he have a fever?" she asked. Immediately she searched her mind for symptoms and illnesses. But Dylan wasn't really a sickly kid. She had absolutely no experience with this. Of course, the first time she was away from home, he'd get sick. She knew it. She shouldn't have left him.

"I couldn't find a thermometer in your house. But he feels warm to me."

Where was the thermometer? She couldn't remember. She sat down on the edge of the bed and closed her eyes. She sought the place she always went to when she was getting ready to go after a bad guy. That calm place where she stored her confidence. And found it. "The thermometer is in my bathroom in the cabinet under the sink."

Taking another deep breath, she started analyzing things. The last time Dylan had a fever he'd been getting new teeth. "Is he drooling a lot, Dad?"

"A little more so than usual, why?"

"He could be teething," Sasha said. "Hang on, I've got a book I want to check."

She set the phone down and ran across the hall to Dylan's room, searching for the copy of the child-rearing book she kept here.

"What's up?" Kane asked, coming into the nursery. "Is everything okay with Dylan?"

"No. Dad's on the phone, Dylan has a fever."

"What other symptoms does he have?" Kane asked her.

She sensed in him the same panic she'd felt. Dylan was the center of his world too. She'd forgotten how to be his partner in this. How to share parenting with Kane. She remembered when they'd first come home from the hospital, and how every night, Kane got up with her to feed Dylan. How every night, Kane had sat at her feet while she'd rocked their son. How every night, Kane and she had smiled over the baby's head, awed that they'd created him.

"I don't know," she said quietly.

She thumbed through the book, trying to find Dylan's age bracket and his symptoms. Kane took the phone from her.

"What's his temperature?" Kane asked her dad. Then, to her, "It's 101.5 degrees, Sasha."

"Is anything else wrong?" Sasha asked. She was scanning the page but there was nothing there about teething. It took about sixty minutes to get to Leeds from the town house if there was no traffic and she ran the Aston at full speed. She'd leave Kane and he could do his cowboy plan. Her baby needed her. God, was she missing something in this book?

Kane asked her dad, listened for a few minutes then covered the mouthpiece. He kept one hand on her shoulder as if he needed some physical contact. She slid her fingers through his so that they were holding hands.

"Other than drooling and reddened gums, nothing's the matter."

"Just teething," she said. She'd been in full-tilt panic mode ready to call an ambulance and make Dylan her number-one priority.

Kane looked a little sheepish. He put his hand over his heart and took a deep breath. This whole situation with Townsend had made them both…uncertain. Insecure about life and what they'd been dealing with. Oh, man, she didn't want to feel like this. She tugged her hand free of his.

Kane watched her with those steady eyes of his. He was a rock. She'd always known that. A stalwart kind of guy she could lean on. But he didn't want a clinging-vine wife and she couldn't live with herself if she clung. But she didn't know how to handle this.

Her stomach hurt and she really needed to hold Dylan. To feel his little body curled in her arms. "Sasha?"

"I'm fine," she said. Get it together, girl. She'd rather face forty men like Tanner than go through what she just had with Dylan. To imagine her little boy sick and…oh, man.

"Was Dad laughing?" she asked.

Kane handed the phone to her. "I'm not laughing," her father said. "It's good to hear the two of you working together."

"Thanks, Dad. I think so too. Temple might be a double agent, so don't trust him. I'm going to be out of contact with A.R.C. for a while, but we'll call every night to sing Dylan to sleep."

"Go back to the part where you won't be in contact with your agency."

"It's a long story, Dad. I'll tell you all about it later."

"Dammit, girl. I didn't raise you—

"But you did. You raised me to follow my own path."

"Now I've got to let you. Is that what you're saying."

"Yes," she said.

"Damn. I hope someday Dylan does the same thing to you."

"I hope so too. Bye, Dad."

She hung up. Kane still stood right next to her. Watching her with his bottomless gray eyes. "Are you sure Dylan's okay?"

"Yes. I'm sure."

He didn't say anything else. He seemed alone and she realized she'd pushed him to a place where they were both in their own separate towers. But of course, he'd gone there willingly.

She didn't analyze anything else. Just went to her husband and held him tight in her arms. He sighed against the crown of her head, hugging her close. Sasha shut her eyes and let Kane soothe away the last bit of panic.

"I'm glad it wasn't anything."

"Me too," he said. They could talk easily about Townsend and would turn to each other when their son was in danger. But when it came to their relationship…

"I'll finish packing," she said. "I'm almost ready to go."

"I *am* ready."

"I want to make sure I don't forget anything." She was a chronic double-checker. She never left her house without going over everything at least twice.

"I'll help you double-check," he said.

"You don't have to," she said.

"Maybe I want to."

As an olive branch it wasn't much. But she felt closer to Kane than she had in a long time. It was as if making love to him last night had re-formed the bonds that they'd both buried deep inside. He followed her across the hall and she was very glad that he was there. Because, despite the fact that she could do everything herself, it was nice to have him nearby.

Sasha's two-way pager beeped, signaling a message was waiting. Kane had gone downstairs to check the arsenal bag she'd brought with her from Leeds. Her dad had packed it so she knew she was ready for anything including an all-out war with Townsend.

She picked up the device and saw the message was from Ano.

Where are you?

I'm out of the game.

Nice try, but you work for me, Nightshade. Meet me at Max's Tattoo on Castle Road at 3:00 p.m.

Sasha e-mailed back. Now that she and Kane were working together as a team and had a plan, she didn't want to mess anything up. Kane had come clean and told her what was going on and Sasha was going to get Anna back.

I'm going rogue.

No, you're not.

Ano, I'm not meeting you.

You need backup and new papers to get into France. Sterling is wanted.

Be right back.

She grabbed her small valise and ran down the stairs. Kane was in the foyer with two bags at his feet. One was a standard U.S. military-type duffel bag— her dad's weapon cache, the other a brown leather piece that matched hers. Temple had given them the bags as wedding gifts.

"Kane, Ano's offering to help us with new papers to get into France."

She wasn't asking permission, she thought. She was the senior officer in charge here. She had to be his equal, she reminded herself. Kane didn't want a clinging vine. Hell, she'd never been a clinging vine and she wasn't about to start now. Meeting Ano made sense because they would need papers to get into France and she didn't have a stash at the town house and doubted Kane did either.

They were both too used to working inside the law. "I'm going to meet her at the tattoo shop to get them."

He gave her an inscrutable look. "Why?"

"Because it makes the most sense. Unless you have disguises hidden somewhere we can wear?"

"I don't. I was planning on…"

"What, killing a customs agent and blazing on through with your gun smoking?"

He gave her a half grin that made her want to smile in return. "Will you stop being so melodramatic? I hadn't considered how we'd get past customs. Maybe we can rent a private plane."

"Did Townsend give you any indication of how he expected you to get over there and meet him?"

"I don't think he cares about my difficulties," Kane said sardonically.

"Meeting Ano makes the best sense. I really think—"

"No, Sasha. I might be on the outside but I'm not going to take an internal HMIA problem to another agency—even yours."

"You're playing right into Townsend's hands. He knows you won't ask for help."

"Why do I need A.R.C. when I have you?"

"Be still my heart." Her two-way beeped again and she glanced down. *Three o'clock Max's.*

Sasha typed in the message to Ano confirming meeting and asking that alternate transportation be left two streets over.

"Trust me on this, Kane. We need help."

"How do you know? You've never done anything that wasn't by the book."

"Yes, I have."

"What? When?"

"Right after we got married. My last case."

"Why am I just now hearing about this?"

"I don't like to talk about it," she said.

"Even with the man you married. Damn, Sasha, that's really nice. So why now?"

She shrugged her shoulders. She wasn't going to tell him that they needed to really trust each other, and even if Kane trusted her until she let him see every facet of the woman he'd married, there couldn't be real honesty between them. And a big part of who she was centered around her mistakes.

"Because you are still not yourself," she said at last.

"Okay, what happened?"

"Let's just say I had a case go personal and really bad."

"How personal?"

"My sister and her son."

"I didn't know you had a sister," Kane said.

She'd never told him. Caroline and Sasha had never really bonded or gotten along. Sasha had seen her sister only twice in the ten years that she'd known Caroline was alive. The meetings had been tense and awkward. Sasha hadn't wanted to see her sister again.

"We weren't close. She grew up with our mother and Dad never told me anything about them."

Kane watched her with his steely gray eyes.

"I had a kidnapping case. I worked it like a pro but when I got to the victims they were...my sister Caroline and her son who was six at the time."

"You have a nephew. Why haven't I met him?"

"Because he lives with his grandparents in Arizona. He doesn't want to see me again. He blames me for his mother's death. His father is out of the picture."

Sasha went to the bench in the hall and sat down, not wanting to look at Kane. He needed to know that she wasn't just guessing at how he felt, she really understood where he was.

Kane sank down besides her, putting a hand on her shoulder. "You didn't kill your sister."

"How do you know?"

"Sasha," he said, shaking his head. "I know you."

"How can you, Kane? I'm not sure I know myself."

He hugged her close to his side and she let him. For the first time since Caroline had died, she let out the emotion she'd bottled up. She told him of the gruesome hours that followed and how she'd abandoned her earpiece at the scene of that abandoned farmhouse and went after the men who'd killed her sister and their bosses.

Kane stroked her arm as she talked about the killing rage that had paralyzed her and made her into some sort of automaton who could just work and not feel.

"But when it was over, the emotions I'd suppressed flooded me. I vowed not to let that happen again."

Kane didn't say anything and she didn't worry about what he thought of her. She'd told him, she realized, to clear the air in her own mind so that she could make a new start of having a relationship with him. And she was the only one who could do that.

"Dylan threw you, didn't he?" Kane said.

"Yes. I was doing well. Newly married, semiretired, but when D was born he brought out all the fears and the seething emotions I thought I'd hidden away."

Sasha pushed to her feet and walked away from Kane because this confession was the hardest. "I had to choose who to care about and I picked D."

"I let you, Sasha. But not again."

Did he mean that he wanted their marriage to work? He picked up the bags and walked out of the house, ending the conversation, and she picked up her bag and followed him out of the house, feeling her two worlds collide and merge. For the first time, she looked beyond the now and saw a future that she actually wanted to live in.

Ten minutes after three, Sasha pulled her car to a stop in the alley behind Castle Road and Max's Tattoo shop. The exterior walls were painted a brilliant royal blue and had bright yellow lettering. Inside there were skulls mounted near the register, and a collection of T-shirts and mugs with some of the more original tattoo designs were for sale.

"Be right with you, mate," a man with spiked hair

said. He wore jeans, a jean vest and no shirt. Down his left arm was a tattoo of a bold-looking dragon. Orly entered from a back room and motioned for Sasha and Kane to follow him.

"These are my friends, Naresh."

The tattoo artist looked up and nodded and then went back to work. They followed Orly through a door to what looked like a storage room. Orly pushed a button and a door slid open to reveal a short flight of stairs that lead to a narrow hallway.

"Is this the highbrow salon where you get your hair done?" Sasha asked as they followed Orly down the hallway.

"Nah. Naresh is my brother."

"I didn't know you had a brother," Sasha said. Orly knew many of her secrets because he'd been her partner and had her back in places where trust wasn't a nice-to-have but a need-to-have.

"Well, you don't know everything, do you?" he said in that smart-ass way of his.

Today seemed to be her day for stepping in it with the men in her life. "I never thought I did. Why are you here?"

"Ano wanted all the players together," Orly said quietly.

Sasha didn't like the sound of that. Ano didn't know the stakes and she might be unintentionally playing into Townsend's hands. Sasha debated pulling back and actually just leaving. There were other ways into France. Both she and Kane knew how to obtain illegal documents. And if worse came to worst,

Sasha could use her dad's military contacts. There were a few men in the military who'd do a favor for the sergeant major, no questions asked.

"Who else is here?" Kane asked.

"Charity, Justice and Temple."

"Why Temple?" Sasha asked. She wasn't too sure that Temple wouldn't punch Kane's lights out when he saw him. Sasha hoped Ano knew what she was doing. But then reminded herself there was a reason why Ano was in charge of A.R.C., and it wasn't a glory position. She'd earned her spot at the top.

"He showed up this morning with Charity and Ano said he was cleared to be here."

Sasha didn't look at Kane but she wanted his take on Temple's presence. Did this mean he wasn't working two sides, or did he have more partners than a naughty college girl who'd just discovered kinky sex?

Kane took her wrist, pulling her to a spot out of earshot of Orly. "I'll do the talking in there."

"Want me to distract them with my feminine wiles?" she asked, feeling as if Kane had forgotten she was a trained agent. Maybe she should have kept her emotional problems to herself back at the town house.

"Too heavy-handed?" he asked, quirking one eyebrow at her.

"Way too over the top. I'm not an idiot. I won't say anything I shouldn't."

"I know that," he said. He leaned forward, resting his forehead against hers. For a moment she caught a flash of vulnerability in his eyes that made her heart ache. Even crazed with rage as he had been that first night on the docks, he'd still been strong. Impenetrable. Very much the alpha male, but tonight he needed his mate and he needed her strength.

"Then why?" she asked softly.

He wrapped her tightly to his chest. She closed her eyes and just breathed in his scent, letting it wash over her. There was something elemental about Kane that always made her feel better. "Dammit, I'm really not sure who to trust and I don't want you getting caught in the backlash."

It was sweet, really, but she was able to handle the backlash. She pushed out of his arms. She was a mate and a partner, he needed to be able to realize that. Or else they had no future together.

"I can manage it."

"Hell, Nightshade. My mind knows that, but my heart says…"

She put her fingers over his lips to keep him from saying anything else. "Mine too. That's why I'm here."

Orly called back to them. "Come on, lovebirds. You're on a short clock."

Sasha moved past Kane and headed toward her partner. "Remind me again why I saved your life, Orly."

He cocked his head to one side and held his hands out to the side, hips canted toward her and pure devilry in his eyes. "You hadn't yet met lover boy here and you were wowed by my spikes."

Sasha laughed. They all entered a small dimly lit room. Ano stood in the corner in the shadows. Charity, Justice and Temple were seated in some garage-sale-reject chairs.

Sasha paused in the doorway, very aware of Kane right behind her.

"Come in," Ano said. "We've been expecting you."

Sasha entered the room, staying close to the door. Kane took up a position on the opposite side.

"Nightshade and Sterling, thanks for coming," Ano said.

Charity handed Sasha a satchel. She opened the top and saw it contained disguises and clothing. As well as Canadian passports. "Thanks for hooking us up," Kane murmured.

"Justine and Orly have a replicated chip that should fool Townsend," Ano said. "On the off chance that it doesn't, I've asked Charity and Temple to go along with you. They'll be your shadows and wait in the wings for you."

"That's not going to work," Kane said. "Townsend's not interested in dealing with a large group of people. He's talking with me because I am on the outside." Kane gave Sasha a look that brooked no argument, and she knew she had a choice. Side with Kane and leave everyone and everything in this room behind or take orders from Ano, let Kane go alone and watch both of them destruct slowly.

Ano kept her eyes on Kane. "Convince me, Sterling."

"I don't have to. You're not my superior and Sasha's made her choice."

"And she's chosen you," Ano said.

"As a matter of fact—yes," Kane replied.

"Well, I'm not letting you go alone. Everyone in

this room agrees that working together will bring the best results. There's a reason you were approached, Sterling," Ano reminded him.

"I understand that far better than you."

Ano turned to Sasha. "Do you understand what he's doing?"

Sasha nodded. Kane was getting his sister back and bringing Townsend in. She hadn't really understood at first, but suddenly she knew it. Kane didn't care what HMIA's agenda was. He'd take what he needed to get the job done.

"As far as he'll know, it won't look like there's more than one man there," Ano said. "I think it might help your case, Sterling, to mention that Nightshade is your wife."

"Why?" Kane demanded.

"She killed Townsend's son when she went in to rescue Perry Ellingham."

"I didn't realize that Townsend's son worked with him," Sasha said, trying to recall the face of the man who may have been Townsend's son.

"Is this the boy that went to school with von Buren's boy?" Kane asked.

"Yes. The same one—Paul Townsend," Justice said. She handed Sasha a surveillance photo of Paul. Immediately she remembered him. He'd been the one to shoot Perry point-blank in the head. She had taken him out.

She'd had no other choice. Her gut had taken over and she'd reacted before he could kill anyone else. There'd been two other hostages that were held with

Perry, and Nightshade had received a commendation for her quick thinking in the field.

Did the death of Townsend's son have anything to do with his new plot to bring down HMIA?

Chapter 14

Truth exists only for each individual when he produces it through his actions.
—Søren Kierkegaard

Two hours later Kane and Sasha boarded the Eurostar—the bullet train—heading to Paris Nord station. They'd entered through a "back door" with papers that approved weapons. Then blended into the crowds in Waterloo station. The trip to Paris would take almost three hours. Kane's communications from Townsend had been spotty.

Townsend favored methods used by intelligence couriers. Kane would receive further instructions from Townsend on the train in the snack car. The instructions would be passed using today's newspaper—the *Guardian*.

Because of that, the entire team was meeting in Paris at a café near the train station. Kane had dyed some silver into his hair so that he looked much as Sasha imagined he might in thirty years. If he lived that long. She wore a long blond wig pulled into a very unflattering ponytail and color contacts. Paired with the long skirt and baggy sweater, she looked frumpy, and, Sasha knew, unmemorable.

Kane sat two rows ahead of her, reading the *Guardian*. With his Japanese suit and beat-up briefcase, he looked like a middle manager off to a conference in France. He'd been very quiet on the ride to the train station.

Ano had pulled her aside to ask Sasha to try one more time to get the chip from Kane. But she knew he wouldn't part with it. Not for her or for Townsend. Her greatest fear was that Kane would force Townsend to kill him to get it.

Orly entered the train with his brother, Naresh, a few minutes after Sasha. Both men, with their spiked-up hair and Naresh's exquisitely drawn tattoos, drew most of the stares in the car. Orly wore an MP3 player on his belt and had the headphones in his ears. Sasha knew that the faux music device was really a two-way radio and that Orly would be in constant communication with A.R.C. headquarters.

They were riding in a second- or coach-class cabin. The seats were silver with a bright yellow stripe down the middle. Sasha's seat was one in a grouping of four that sat facing each other. Kane was seated in a pair that faced forward.

Orly and Naresh moved toward the back of the car in another four-group where two college-age girls were seated. Sasha knew she was too far away to really be sure, but she sensed Orly's joy at his luck. The man was nothing if not a first-class flirt.

Nightshade lifted a copy of French *Vogue* and skimmed it while keeping a weather eye on the car. Before entering a country, she liked to refresh herself in the native language. She'd worked a case once in rural south France and had become almost native in her speaking. But that was a long time ago.

A mother with a stroller, diaper bag and cranky child boarded the train just minutes before departure. And headed for Sasha's seating group. The mom hit one man in the head with her diaper bag. Sasha watched her struggle for a second, then got out of her seat to help.

"I'll fold up the stroller for you while you get the baby settled."

"Thanks, Nick has had a long day."

"My son is the same way. Traveling is not really his thing. He hates to have his routine messed with."

"That's my Nick to a tee. Thank you for helping out. I'm Marla by the way."

"No problem. I'm Didi."

The woman stowed her diaper bag and settled into a window seat with Nick. He appeared to be about Dylan's age and looked on the world with the same wide eyes that her son did. The mom took a small container of snacks from her purse and fed them to her son.

She'd been away less than a week, but it seemed so much longer. She couldn't wait to wrap this up and get back home.

The conductor came through and collected their tickets and they were on the way. Sasha leaned back in the seat and watched the passengers in the car. Twenty minutes into the ride, Kane stood and stretched, then left the main car.

Sasha stretched her legs. "I'm going to get a drink, you want anything?" she asked Marla.

"I can wait for the snack cart," the woman said.

"Okay."

Sasha entered the cafeteria car a few minutes after Kane. She stood in line between two Asian youths who spoke in their native tongue. Sasha sorted through languages until she recognized it as Taiwanese. She eavesdropped on their conversation, watching while Kane ordered a combo snack, then stood at one of the tables in the car to eat.

Sasha ordered a soft drink, an orange and a bag of trail mix. She stood at a table close to Kane's and calmly peeled her orange. The snack car wasn't crowded but there was a steady stream of people in and out. Sasha took her time with the orange, watching a man with a long black raincoat enter from the opposite end.

He ordered the same combo as Kane and went to stand at her husband's table. Sasha finished her orange and slid into the phone booth at the opposite end so that she could keep an eye on Kane. She picked up the phone and pretended to dial.

But she noted that the man had laid a copy of today's *Guardian* on the opposite side of the table from Kane's. Sasha saw Kane pick up the other man's paper, tuck it under his arm.

Satisfied that the drop had been made and that Kane was safe, she returned to the coach cabin. Marla and Nick weren't in their seats. But Orly walked by and dropped what looked like a receipt on the floor. Sasha waited a few beats, made sure no one was watching and bent to retrieve the note.

Public toilets—10.

Sasha glanced at her watch and noted the time. Kane returned to his seat and tucked the paper into his briefcase. He left the fastening on the right side unlocked, which was a signal to her. The drop had gone as planned and everything was in place.

Sasha used the vocal tap code to let Kane know she'd received his message. The vocal tap code was a series of coughs, throat clearing, sniffing, hacking and sneezing that had been invented for POWs to use. A.R.C. had found it an easy way to communicate in public places as well.

Marla returned in the middle of the sneezing. "Are you okay?"

"I have allergies." Sasha checked her watch and saw that it was almost time to meet Orly. "Excuse me."

She made her way to the public rest rooms. As agreed to before they'd arrived at the station, Sasha went to the second facility on the right and entered it, closing the door but not locking it.

Orly entered a few minutes later, closing and locking the door.

"Everything's going smoothly. Kane picked up the info without any problem."

"Good," Orly said. "Because Temple is missing."

"Where'd we lose him?"

"Inside Waterloo station," he told her.

"Where's Charity?" Sasha asked.

"Still at Waterloo. She's going to catch a flight and meet us in Paris."

Sasha returned to her seat only to find that Kane was no longer in the cabin. Seemed like everything was going from sugar to shit in the blink of an eye.

Sasha exited the train at Paris Nord station. The next time she got her hands on her husband he was going to have a lot of explaining to do. Kane hadn't returned to his seat for the rest of the trip.

She'd paged him twice on the two-way while Marla had taken the ever-cranky Nick for a walk, but Kane hadn't responded. She was worried about Kane and not sure she'd done the right thing in trusting him, trusting Ano and letting so many people know exactly what was going on.

Bruce Temple's being missing also bothered her. She still wasn't sure whose side he was on. If he was working against her and had anything to do with Anna Sterling being taken, then Sasha would be first in line to make him pay. But her gut kept telling her that Temple was a friend.

She had a million questions and no answers. She'd already warned her dad about Temple, but as soon as she got out of the station she planned to call and make sure that Dylan was still safe. The time difference between London and Paris was only an hour.

She entered the women's rest room, disposed of the baggy skirt and sweater. Pulled off the wig and fluffed her curly hair. She took out her makeup bag and removed the contacts so that her own brown was visible. She applied a dark shade of red lipstick.

She reversed her purse so that it now looked as if it was made of sleek Italian leather instead of canvas. The bag had been designed to change sizes. She pulled out her blazer and zipped the inner shell of the bag into itself until it was the size of a decent handbag. She put the small earpiece of her two-way mike in her ear.

"Testing," she said quietly.

"Gotcha," Orly said.

"Any signal from Kane?"

"Negative."

"See you in five," Sasha said. She took the Glock from the ankle holster and moved it to one at the small of her back. She pulled on her blazer and left the stall.

She entered the crowded Paris station and moved quickly through the terminal toward the rendezvous point—a restaurant that was a decent walk from the station on rue Belzunce.

Leaning against the wall near the rest rooms, she waited. Kane would have to ditch his disguise and come out a new man. Casually she surveyed everyone in the crowd. One guy winked at her and another one made a move toward her. She shook her head to discourage him and then spotted Kane moving toward the opposite exit.

She took a spot in the crowd and followed him. He'd rinsed the silver out of his hair and it was now slicked back. He wore a pair of tight jeans and a black T-shirt.

"Orly, I'm on Sterling. Go to the rendezvous without me."

"Gotcha."

Kane stepped out into the deepening night of Paris. Sasha watched him move with no hesitation away from the station on rue de Dunkerque. Sasha didn't know where Kane was going. But Chez Michel, the restaurant where they were to meet the team, was in the other direction.

"Nightshade, you're not authorized to follow. Return to rendezvous point."

"Negative, Orly."

"Relaying."

"Bite me, Orly, I'm following him regardless of what Ano orders."

"Gotcha. Be careful. I'll stay loose."

Kane paused to check out the window of a shop. Checking for tails, no doubt. She wasn't sure what he was up to. Sasha had about ten seconds to duck out of view. The man who'd met Kane in the cafeteria car paused as well.

Kane had more than one person following him. She took her two-way pager from her pocket and sent him a message, letting him know she'd clear his back trail for him.

If she didn't know him as well as she did, she wouldn't have noticed the way he checked the pager screen. He nodded his head. Sasha prepared to go to work.

"Kane's being followed. I'm going to help him flush his tails and we'll both meet you in fifteen."

"Gotcha. Need backup?"

"Negative, Orly."

"There are two A.R.C. operatives in the area who are moving to intercept. Ano repeats her call for you to drop back."

"When the other operatives are in place I will. Remind Ano that I know what I'm doing."

"Gotcha, boss lady."

Kane headed straight into the Hôtel Gare du Nord Trudaine. Two men followed Kane in. One of them was the guy from the train station. Sasha entered. Kane was in line at the reception desk. The other man kept moving through the lobby toward the bank of elevators.

A hand snaked out and grabbed her around the waist. Sasha started to elbow him, when she recognized those deep chocolate eyes and black hair. Vincent Lorenzi aka Vengeance. He was an A.R.C. operative that she'd worked with a time or two before. "*Bonjour,* sexy! How was the train?" he murmured, his French perfect.

What the hell was Vinny doing here? She didn't know how Ano had gotten him in place so quickly. She hadn't been expecting him.

"*Bondé*—couldn't find a seat anywhere. Didn't expect to see you here."

He gave her a quick kiss. "Couldn't wait to see you—*tu me manques, n'est-ce pas, chérie?* Missed you too much. If you're checking in, why not get *une chambre pour moi aussi* while I take care of business?" he said. Like they were lovers who'd been apart too long.

Let him take care of business. Ano was getting a little pushy about making sure she was in charge. That would be the day. He tilted her head back and rubbed his lips along her jaw, whispering words against her skin. "The man you're following is dangerous."

"I like danger."

He laughed and hugged her close for a minute. "This won't take me any time at all."

She realized that one of her weaknesses was always having to do everything herself. Kane was getting closer to the front of the line. And Vinny needed to go if he was going to catch their friend from the train. "Okay. Be careful. Hurry back."

"I will."

She got on the reception line right behind Kane. He held himself stiffly and she knew that he didn't trust Vinny. She wanted to reassure Kane but was still ticked off about his disappearing act earlier. Let him worry about Vinny for a while longer.

Sasha stood a discreet distance from Kane but close enough to hear him ask for a package for Monsieur Beauchamps. The clerk disappeared into the back room and returned a few minutes later with a brown-wrapped package.

Kane gave her a curt nod and left the building.

Sasha abandoned up any pretense of checking in and followed Kane out. But he'd already disappeared off the street. She checked the foot traffic to the left, then the right, and couldn't spot him. She started walking slowly back toward the train station. A hand grabbed her arm as she passed an alley and pulled her off the street.

Kane waited for her. But the look in his eyes said he wasn't too pleased.

"What are you doing?" he asked, pinning her between his rock-hard body and the cold brick wall.

Sasha took a moment to savor his closeness before biting him on the neck and pulling back. "Following my husband... Remember, we agreed to work together."

Bending his head, he scraped his teeth along the length of her neck and suckled her earlobe. "That's not what we agreed. I said no more secrets. Not you tailing me."

Sensual shivers raced down her body. She knew anyone walking by would see two lovers seeking a moment's privacy on a busy street. But she was having a hard time keeping the fact that this was a charade present in her mind.

"If you hadn't pulled your invisible-man stunt, I wouldn't have had to follow you," she said, scoring her nails down his chest. She could feel his muscles ripple in response through the thin layer of his T-shirt.

Taking her hands in both of his, he raised them and

took her mouth in a kiss that was so dominant and forceful, she wanted to surrender her will to him. But she knew she couldn't let him win at this game. And he was toying with her. Touching her in the ways he knew she liked. Because most men feared her physically, it was a turn-on for her to feel like the weaker one. And Kane played that beautifully, shackling both of her wrists in his hands and holding them above her head against the cold brick wall.

"I'm not going to report in to you, Nightshade, before I make a move."

"You two are turning me on," Orly said in her ear.

"Bugger off, mate," she said under her breath.

"Talking to me?"

Sasha shook her head, forcing her concentration off the sexual desire that pooled in the center of her body. Her hips rocked forward against him. And he groaned deep in his throat. She sighed and then forcibly pushed him away from her. "Orly."

"What?" Orly said.

"Tell him to get stuffed," Kane said.

"You can pick a fight with him later," Sasha said. "I know how tiring constant monitoring can be. But when you work with a team, it's important that all the team members stay informed."

"Wow, that was a mouthful. What are you trying to tell me?" he asked, shoving his hands through his hair. She noticed he was still slightly aroused. If the stakes in this operation weren't so high, she'd enjoy playing with Kane like this.

"Temple disappeared in London before we got on

the train," she said, doing her yoga breathing and searching for the kind of serenity that she never really could keep.

"Damn."

"Charity took a Virgin Express flight and is waiting for us at the Chez M," she said. She hoped that Charity had some solid information on Temple.

"Then by all means, let's not keep her waiting," he said sardonically.

"What did you get from the desk clerk?" she asked as they left the alleyway. She didn't see any sign of the man who'd been following Kane, or any sign of Vinny.

"Hopefully the location where Anna's being held. I haven't had a chance to look." He kept her tucked close to his side and she wondered what his contact had said to him to make him this…overprotective. She stepped out of his sheltering embrace. He gave her one of those inscrutable looks of his and sighed but didn't reach for her to pull her back.

"Why not?" she asked.

"Because someone was following me."

She raised both eyebrows. She glanced behind them. The crowd on the street was thin and not ample cover for anyone who was trying to tail them. So far, none of the faces she'd seen sparked a memory or recognition. "I was following you."

"Exactly."

She punched him in the shoulder. "Sterling, you make me crazy."

He caught her fist and brushed a kiss against the back of her knuckles. "I try."

She tried to ascertain if Kane was playing to an unseen audience or if he was sincere. He seemed almost lighthearted and, after seeing the dark storm clouds in his eyes for so long, she wanted to rejoice. But she knew this wasn't real. This was some surreal world she'd stepped into where things seemed okay but they weren't.

She rubbed the back of her neck. It was the case. She'd reached that part where real life ceased to exist and the only reality she felt was the moment she was living in. It didn't help that she was here with Kane. If it had been Vinny holding her hand and kissing her, she could remember it was all an act, but with Kane…she'd never been able to pretend with him.

He hailed a cab and gave the address for Chez Michel. Sasha held herself stiffly as the small car careened around corners. Kane snaked his arm around her shoulders and pulled her flush against his body.

"Every time I think I've got you under my spell you slip away," he said softly.

"I didn't realize you were trying to enchant me." But she had. From their first date until the moment he'd moved out of their house in Leeds, Kane had always been a romantic. He'd swept her off her feet by doing the unexpected and seeing past the barriers she used to protect herself from feeling too much. Only later had he stopped seeing past those walls.

"It's the only way I can think of to hold you," he

said. The streetlights flashed by, but in that instant his face was illuminated and she saw a truth in his eyes that scared her to the pit of her soul.

"Why do you have to hold me?" she asked, trying to quell the panic rising deep inside. Panic she knew stemmed directly from the fact that she wanted to be held by Kane. Only Kane.

"It's the only time I feel like you're mine."

His words made her heart ache. There was no way to reassure him. No way to make him understand that the harder he tried to hold her down, the more fiercely she'd fight to be free. Kane scared her not so much because of the way he tried to tie her to him, but because when she was wrapped up in him and lying next to him, she didn't want to leave.

"Don't do this to me now."

"Sorry. Who was that *David* kissing you in the lobby?"

"That's Vengeance. Ano sent him."

"Is she in Paris?" he asked. She saw something else in his eyes. A question that said had he pushed her too hard and she had no answer to either question.

"I don't know," she said. And she didn't know. They couldn't go on like this. It would be better if he'd really go rogue and get out of her hair so she could concentrate on what she did best without having his distracting presence nearby. But she knew if he did leave, she'd follow him. Because something ethereal bound them together. And that thing was stronger than Nightshade and Townsend and Ano. It was stronger than anything Kane or she had ever faced. Sasha's only hope was that they both found a way to survive with that bond intact.

Chez Michel was located in an out-of-the-way neighborhood near the Gare du Nord. A stylish crowd filled the tables. Sasha pulled Kane to a stop in the shadowy area outside the door.

"We're here," Sasha said to Orly.

"Come straight back, we're using a room at the top of the stairs," he said.

She took Kane's hand in hers and led him through the restaurant. They climbed the stairs and entered the room. Charity and Temple sat at one table, while Orly and Justice were in another corner of the room working over a small computer screen.

Temple's nose was swollen and there was a small bandage on his forehead. His clothing looked the worse for wear. His gun sat on the table and his hand tightened on it when he saw Kane.

"What the hell happened to you?" Sasha asked, drawing his attention.

He stood up, knocking the ladder-back chair out of the way. He held his gun loosely in his right hand and though he spoke to her, his eyes never left Kane. "I had a visit from one of *his* friends."

"Which ones?" Sasha asked. Behind her, Kane moved a pace to the left and she glanced over her shoulder and saw he had loosened his jacket. Probably to make grabbing his gun easier. Great, just what she needed—two macho men trying to gun each other down.

Temple approached them. There was wildness in his eyes. This case was running everyone ragged. There was too much they still didn't know and, though no one said it out loud, time was running out for Anna. Townsend was playing his little game with Kane but he wouldn't be patient for too much longer.

She knew Temple was ready for a confrontation and she suspected that Kane was too.

Sasha blocked Temple's path. If they wanted to beat the crap out of each other—she'd let them, but not right now. Now they needed to analyze whatever information Kane had been given and run a few more tests on the chip that Orly and Justice were working on. "Aggression doesn't solve anything."

"I disagree, Sasha. It'll make me feel bloody good," Temple said.

"I don't need you in this," Kane said. Wrapping his hand around her upper arm, he pulled her out of the way. Sasha had had enough of both of them. She brought her heel down on his instep and heard his groan of pain. Followed it up with a front jab that Kane avoided. He narrowed his eyes at her.

She didn't care how ticked off he was. Acting like an idiot wasn't going to help anyone. Satisfied she'd gotten through to Kane, she turned to Temple.

With a roundhouse kick, she connected with Temple's stomach. He groaned. He blocked her front jab and then lifted his hands to shoulder level.

"Stop it. We're not doing something stupid and bullheaded. You two want to have a pissing contest, do it later. Right now, we have to stay focused on Anna."

"I think you made your point," Kane said quietly.

"Agreed. We'll take this up later," Temple said.

They all crossed to the table. Sasha took a seat, as did Temple. Kane stood behind her with his arms crossed over his chest.

"When I exited customs at Waterloo, two guys came up behind me and took me into a small custodian closet. They tried to rough me up."

"Looks like they succeeded," Kane said drolly.

"Then they warned me to stay out of Sterling's way and left."

Sasha tried to analyze what had happened. Could Shubert have sent the men? He wouldn't know that Temple was working with A.R.C. on this. Or did he?

She pulled a small notebook from her purse and jotted down the date and time of the incident and then what Temple had said. As soon as they were done here, she was going to contact Ano and get her to find out what Shubert was doing. Was he keeping Temple and Sterling apart or was it someone else in the organization?

Kane leaned over Sasha's shoulder. "Can you describe the men?"

Temple nodded. He gave hair and eye color. "About my height and weight," he continued. "They had training, that's for sure."

"Justice, can you access the database from here?"

"Which one, Nightshade?"

"Agents and known terrorists who might work for Townsend."

"Yes, I'll get it, but it'll take me at least ten minutes."

"No problem. Temple, will you look through it and see if you can ID those men?"

"Yes. Has Townsend recruited anyone else from our organization? Because those guys were trained like we are."

Sasha looked at Kane and he met her stare. She knew what he was asking her. Should he trust Temple? She shrugged.

From the beginning she'd had a hard time putting Temple in Townsend's camp. It didn't mean she was right about him. But her gut had always been right, even when she'd doubted it.

"He's trying to recruit me, Temple."

"Bloody hell. I wondered if that wasn't it. Why didn't you say something?"

Kane pulled out the remaining chair and sprawled back in it. He rubbed the bridge of his nose and she knew that trusting another person wasn't something that Kane did easily. Not even with those close to him. Temple had been like a brother to him but still Kane was reluctant to share what he knew. It had been the same with her. He was a control freak, she realized, wondering why she hadn't noticed it before.

"There's a leak at HMIA," he said at last.

Temple leaned back in his chair. "You think it's me?"

Kane didn't deny that he'd suspected Temple but he didn't accuse him either. The beating Temple had sustained could be an elaborate ruse or it could have been for real. "I don't know who it is."

"Hell. Why is A.R.C. involved?" Temple asked.

"Thanks to Sasha here. She suggested that Townsend wouldn't expect the agencies to collaborate. Working together, we might be able to stop him before he ruins the cooperation we have between the global intelligence agencies. That's why he asked for the list."

"What about Anna?" Temple asked.

"He really has her." Kane pulled a thin brown envelope from under his shirt and opened it. He pulled out a piece of paper and read the message.

"Next stop Marseilles. A hotel called Le Petit Nice. I have to be there by noon tomorrow."

"Will the chip be ready by then?"

"Should be," Orly said.

"I'm not betting my sister's life on that. Yes or no, can we use the chip you've created?"

Orly took a deep breath. Tempers in the room were thin and prone to snapping. Sasha didn't need this. None of this was bringing them closer to finding Anna and capturing Townsend.

"Go cool down."

"Don't push me, Nightshade."

"Don't you push me, Sterling."

He gave her an ice-cold look and walked away. "Let me talk to Orly. You and Temple work things out or kill each other. Right now, I don't care which."

Chapter 15

Whether or not it is clear to you, no doubt the Universe is unfolding as it should.

—Max Erhrmann

Charity had arranged for food to be brought up. Sasha's stomach rumbled when she smelled the escargot in garlic sauce. She took a sip of the Burgundy and went to the computer area that Orly and Justice had set up.

Justice had a second computer up and running and was downloading pictures from the database for Temple to look at. The databases she accessed were exclusive to A.R.C. and not usually ones that they let other operatives see.

"Did you clear this with Ano?" Sasha asked.

"She's in a meeting but I left her a message. I was thinking about what you said about Townsend expecting us to all guard our proprietary information. The only way to bring him down is to work together."

She smiled at Justice. "I made sense when I said that?"

"To me at least."

Justice and Orly used the real list with the real code names. But then scrambled the code names by four. So that the new list was skewed. She thought the list would work because when she looked at it she had no idea which were the real code names. The only catch would be if Townsend knew operatives and their code names already.

"I don't like the idea of just randomly sorting the list. The list is still dangerous if he has the names of all the operatives."

"Orly has devised a virus that will let Townsend view the list for up to ten minutes. If he attempts to alter or save the list, the virus kicks in immediately. That might pose a problem for Sterling."

Sasha had no doubt that Townsend would kill Kane instantly if a virus started running on his computer. "Orly has devised a way to disguise the virus so that on the screen all Townsend sees is the list while the virus does the work in the back."

"Yes. But it might take longer than we have," Justice told her.

"Keep working on it. Tell me what the virus does."

"Just wipes his hard drive. I programmed it to

save and send all the information he has on the computer to us."

"Nice thinking, Orly."

He winked at her. "Thanks, boss lady."

The second computer beeped. Justice swiveled around to read the screen. "The database is ready for Temple. We need the HMIA interface for the beginning."

Sasha nodded, knowing this was the moment when Kane would either be a team player or everything they'd been planning would fall through. "I'll take care of it."

Justice signaled Temple, who came over to her station. Then Sasha turned to Orly. "Why don't you take a break and go eat?"

"You need to rest too," Orly said as he pulled her to one side of the room. Sasha kept a close eye on all the players but especially Kane. He was talking to Charity and, for all intents and purposes, everything seemed to be going well.

"I can't. Not yet," she said. She wanted to keep her eye on everyone. Wanted to make sure that the tension that had nearly sprung out of control between Temple and Sterling didn't return. She was the only one with a vested interest in both sides of this team.

"You can't do this alone," Orly said quietly. He patted his pockets, searching for a cigarette. He took out the pack and lit up.

"I'm not trying to." She hated when Orly got all philosophical on her. She liked him better as the sexy computer whiz who could charm his way into any woman's bed. When he got serious, she started worrying because he didn't do it often and, dammit, he was usually right.

"Yes, you are. The same way you always do it. I'm here, Kane's here, let us shoulder some of this burden."

Letting go of the control seemed logical, but she wasn't wired that way. There were too many variables that couldn't be controlled and Sasha had always just focused on what she could keep under the leash. And this team was one of those things.

"I can't, Orly."

He took a deep drag on the cigarette. He blew out a series of smoke rings and she knew he was trying to distract her. "Don't you trust us?"

Trust, damn. It seemed no matter where she went that one thing dogged her heels. Trust wasn't so much about anyone else, Sasha realized. But about herself. She had to let go of her own authority to trust someone else. And she didn't believe in herself enough to do that. "Of course I do. I guess I want to protect you both from…"

She couldn't say anything else, wouldn't confess the fears that plagued her at night. Fears driven by the dark side of her soul that she'd let loose once. That side tormented her with visions of her darkest fears. Fears that those she cared for would be put into jeopardy and none of her careful plans would be enough to save them.

Only the dark burning anger that wasn't ruled by the logical part of her mind would be enough to save them. That was her worst fear but there was no way she was revealing that to Orly.

"What? We're both able to protect ourselves," he said. He finished his cigarette and stubbed it out. Then he flicked the butt toward the waste can in the corner.

"I know that. But you both have vulnerabilities and I'm trying to keep you from exposing those."

He watched her steadily and she kept her expression hard and steely. She was a tough-as-nails agent who could beat a confession out of a bad guy. The only problem was, she was also the mom of a toddler, and Orly had seen her as such. Orly knew that she had a soft side and he wasn't above using that knowledge.

"You have them too, Nightshade."

"You're supposed to pretend you don't see them," she said quietly. It would make life so much easier for everyone if weak spots weren't visible to the naked eye. For the most part she was able to pretend hers didn't exist, but she'd spent the majority of her train ride worrying about Kane. Fearing that he'd done something that she wouldn't be able to rescue him from.

"Why, does that make them go away?" he asked.

"No. But it makes it easier to ignore them. Speaking of ignoring—where's Naresh?"

"With his girlfriend. He's going to stay in Paris a few days and then head home."

"I would have liked to talk to him."

"Why?"

"To get some good blackmail stories from your childhood."

"There aren't any," Orly replied.

"Why don't I believe that?"

"Because you have a nasty, suspicious mind."

"You're right, I do. It's one of my better qualities."

"Your big heart is the only one you have to concentrate on, Nightshade. That's the thing that sets you apart from other agents. It's your biggest strength."

"Sometimes I think that caring is my biggest weakness."

"Ah, well, it might be. Your strength is always a double-edged sword."

Orly straightened from the wall and walked away, leaving Nightshade to think about what he'd said. She closed her eyes and searched deep inside herself for answers, but she couldn't find them and that made her uneasy. There was a niggling sensation at the back of her neck that warned she was overlooking some angle that was important.

Kane and Sasha were booked on an 8:00 a.m. flight from Paris's Charles de Gaulle Airport to Marseilles. They'd all eaten and taken catnaps. Orly still worked at the computer and Temple and Justice crowded around him as he ran different versions of the virus, trying different variables and hoping to come up with something in the next hour or so that Kane could use instead of the real list.

Nightshade was clearly the officer in command and no one had questioned her right to lead on this case. Even Kane seemed to have resolved himself to being part of a team.

"Shubert refused to see me," Ano said via the two-way secured radio.

Sasha leaned back in her chair. She wondered if Kane had talked to his boss. Had the time for communication ended? "He could be afraid to let you know too many of their secrets."

"He could be an ass."

"Ano, be nice," Sasha said. They didn't need Shubert. The team they'd pulled together using operatives from different organizations was a strong one and Nightshade had no doubts that they'd find Anna Sterling and bring Townsend in.

"Can't. The man really pissed me off. I'd pull you off of the case except I know you wouldn't return without the Sterling girl."

She thought about that for a minute. It was true that she would keep the team in place and continue to move forward. Ano gave them all a certain amount of leeway that other agencies didn't afford their field operatives. She liked to call it the Renegade Plan. "You wouldn't have called me if you wanted it any other way."

"Something changed in your voice. Are you okay?" Ano asked. Sasha pictured her boss sitting in her big executive chair with her feet propped on the desk.

She wasn't sure what Ano had heard. Maybe it was the new peace she'd found. Or it could be the quiet zone that she got into whenever things were about to start hopping. "Yes. I'm just tired."

"It's not fatigue," Ano said.

"Maybe it's surprise. I didn't know you'd pulled Vinny in to work with us." He still hadn't reported in, which didn't worry Nightshade. Vengeance was one of the toughest operatives they had. His specialty was infiltrating some of the nastiest drug rings in Europe. So this wasn't his usual case, but she was glad he'd been brought in.

"I'm covering all the bases. We need people who weren't in London. Von Buren left for Marseilles last night."

"Is he booked at the same hotel as Kane?" she asked, making notes on the pad at her elbow. She glanced up and met Kane's eyes, signaling for him to come to her.

He dropped his hand on the table and sauntered over to her. She handed him an earpiece. "Sterling's on the line as well."

"I haven't been able to get information on where von Buren is staying. Our records show he has a house in Toulon which isn't too far," Ano told them.

"As soon as we get to Le Petit Nice we'll know more. I'm not even sure we'll be staying at the hotel," Kane offered.

"According to our travel database, you have a reservation. We've made one for Nightshade at the same hotel," Ano replied.

"Has Vengeance checked in?" Sasha asked.

"About thirty minutes ago. He was en route to your location."

Sasha nodded. "Did he find anything?"

"He took out the man who'd been following Sterling and then questioned him at the local police station."

"And?" Kane prompted.

"Not much. He's a businessman who is sticking to his story of being in the wrong place at the wrong time. He says he wasn't following anyone," Ano told him.

Sasha frowned at this news. "Coincidence?"

"Not by a long shot. He works for a small company that is owned by von Buren's corporation."

"That doesn't mean von Buren's definitely in this. We don't have any proof," Sasha protested.

"We got some yesterday," Ano corrected. "Otto von Buren and Paul Townsend didn't just go to the same school, they were best friends. They alternated spending holidays with the Townsends and the von Burens. The families were definitely connected."

"I wonder what happened."

"Well, Paul went to work for Townsend and he wasn't as successful as his father."

Sasha shivered, thinking of the fact that she'd killed a man with friends and family. The logical part of her mind knew that all the people she fired on had relationships, but in the moment on a case it was easy to see them as a target, not a real person. And this was the first time she'd had to confront the results of doing her job.

"So what happened?" Sasha asked.

"Townsend's wife, Dora, left him," Ano replied. "Otto had continued contact with Townsend until six months ago when he disappeared."

"Which coincides with your moving out of our

house. Did you start setting this up then?" Sasha asked Kane.

He pushed the mute button on the phone. "My moving out had nothing to do with work and everything to do with the fact that I couldn't keep living with an automaton. I wanted you to be the woman I married. The woman who laughed easily and who seduced me all the time."

"Oh. I…"

He covered her lips with his thumb. "I like this new you, Sasha."

"I can't guarantee that I won't retreat again," she warned.

"I *can* guarantee that I won't let you."

"You two still there?" Ano asked.

Kane took them off mute. "Yes, we're here. Shubert didn't approach me until about three months ago. Everyone knew I was displeased with the ruling on my last case."

"He suggested you get good and angry and get yourself suspended," Sasha said.

"Not in those exact terms, but yeah, that's what happened."

"When did Townsend first approach you?" Ano asked.

"Didn't we already do this dance?" Kane said.

"Humor me. Sometimes we can pick up things from hearing the same information again," Ano said.

"Two months ago I was suspended. About a week later I got a note inviting me to go to Café de Paris and give my name to the bouncer at the VIP room."

"And that's when you met von Buren?"

"No. He was in the room but I never talked to him. My instructions were to go to the bar and order a martini—shaken not stirred."

"Nice. Very James Bond-like."

"I was doubtful anything would come of it, but ten minutes after my drink arrived I was taken out the back door and to a limo."

"Please tell me you didn't get in," Sasha said.

"Of course I got in."

"Idiot. You could have been killed," Sasha said accusingly.

"Clearly I wasn't."

"You're a father now, Kane."

"Later, Nightshade," Ano said. "What happened next?"

"Townsend was in that limo. He said he'd heard things weren't going too well in my career and if I was interested in continuing my work, he had an opportunity for me."

"What did he offer you?" Ano asked. She was in top security-officer mode right now. Sasha wondered if a part of Ano was curious about what kind of offer someone would receive to betray a lifetime of honor and duty.

Sasha couldn't look at Kane. She didn't know this man. A man that a known criminal would approach. She knew he was doing it for his case. That his own boss had thought he was right for this job meant that Kane had to be dissatisfied somewhere.

Kane rubbed the back of his neck. It was one thing

to discuss this offer with her but another to talk openly with the director of an intelligence agency that wasn't his own. "Just a lucrative job, freedom from chain of command and a chance to do what I do best."

"Well, what you do best is solve crimes for Her Majesty," Sasha said, wanting to make it clear to Ano and to Kane that he wasn't a rogue.

Kane gave her a quick squeeze. "That's right."

"When you arrive in Marseilles we'll have a car waiting for you. Sterling, once you've checked in at Le Petit Nice, rendezvous with Nightshade."

"Where are we going from there?" Sasha asked.

"To Toulon. It's sixty-seven kilometers from Marseilles and it's an active naval port. Ships are in and out of there all the time. Back from the harbor is Le Petit Chicago—it's a gritty area we think Townsend is operating out of."

"Any ideas where?" Kane asked.

"I'm sending Vengeance and another operative, Trinity, to do some recon while you play Townsend's game. They'll meet you at place des Trois Dauphins near the fern-lined fountain at 2100 hours."

Nine o'clock. "Anything else?"

"That's it for now. Be careful. If you can locate and retrieve Anna Sterling without having to confront Townsend, do it. We want him, but get the girl out first."

"Will do."

"I'm going to try to contact Shubert," Kane said, moving toward a far corner of the room.

Sasha didn't say anything, but went to Justice where she worked on one of the computers. "We need to know more about von Buren's corporation and normal travel. Does he have a house in Marseilles?"

Justice started typing. Sasha sank into a chair next to her friend and just watched the information coming up on the screen. "His wife has property in Nice and they have a small house in Monte Carlo but I don't see anything in Marseilles."

"Anywhere else on the Côte d'Azur?"

"Give me a minute. I'm e-mailing some other files to you. Use Orly's computer and catch up on your reading while I search for real estate."

"Okay. Don't forget to use Otto's name as well."

"Hans's son?"

"Yes."

Sasha went to Orly's computer and read the files that Justice had found on von Buren's corporation. A multinational import/export business that had been investigated seven times and each time come back as clean. Sasha knew that for the company to have been investigated that many times, von Buren had to have been doing something illegal. Something that they shouldn't have been doing. And given his business, that meant smuggling or illegal trade.

A.R.C. never did the investigations because they were troubleshooters and not officially sanctioned by any one government, though they worked routinely for the U.S. She ran into a firewall when she tried to get the official reports. "Orly, I need you."

She heard his chair scrape across the wooden floor

and a few minutes later, he was at her side. "What do you need?"

"I want to read the official reports of the von Buren investigations."

He ran his hand through his spiked-up hair and his eyes took on that glazed look that meant he was already puzzling out how to do it. "It'll take a few minutes."

"Hey, I have until eight."

"Well, move your sweet ass, boss lady. I need to be in the driver's seat."

She shook her head but got up and let Orly work his magic. She walked over to Justice, who glanced up from her computer and gave her a good glare. "Don't ask."

"I think I'll go get some coffee, want some?" she asked. Justice wasn't the friendliest person under the best of circumstances; clearly the computer wasn't giving her the information she wanted.

"No. I'll call when I have something."

Sasha wished she smoked. It would give her something to do to pass the time while she waited. Technology made things go faster when investigating but there were still periods like this one where you just had to wait it out.

Temple and Charity had moved their chairs to face the door. She thought about joining them but decided against it. What she really needed was some fresh air and time to think.

She was changing. She felt it deep inside. She couldn't go back to Leeds and be content the way she'd been before. But she couldn't be gone like this from Dylan either. She missed her son. He brought out the best in her as a person. He gave her the excuse she needed to really let her emotions go.

But this was her calling. This was what she was meant to do and where she was meant to be. She sank down on the floor with her back against the wall.

Kane sat down next to her. "What's going through your mind?"

"Just playing with the facts of the case," she said as he handed her a cup of coffee. She took a sip and then handed the mug back to him. He took a sip from the same place she had.

"What did Shubert say?" she asked.

"That he'd have my ass for bringing another intelligence organization into our mess. We discussed the matter and he agreed to speak to Ano."

"Good. She can be reasonable."

"Ha. The women of A.R.C. are never reasonable unless you agree to do what they say."

"We're usually right."

"I'll give you that."

He handed her the coffee again and she took another sip. "I'm tired."

Kane put his arm around her shoulder. "Rest here."

She tried to but one question kept surfacing in her mind. "Why'd you get into that limo, Kane?"

He sighed and she glanced up at him. He had his head tipped back against the wall. Stubble covered his jaw and part of his neck.

"I was pissed off."

"At me?"

"You, Shubert…hell, probably everyone. I'd been drinking and I thought what the hell. I was ready for a fight."

"You got more than a fight, didn't you?"

"Hell, yes. Do you want to hear that I screwed up? I did, Sasha. I'm not like you…I don't turn off my emotions and make all my decisions out of some logical part of my brain. I'm human and I fucking make mistakes."

He pushed to his feet and stalked away and she sat there holding the cup of coffee and wondering how the hell their relationship had gotten so screwed up. She was human and her heart was breaking because she'd ruined a good man.

Chapter 16

Listen, or your tongue will keep you deaf.
                    —Native North American proverb

There was a new tension in the room. Sasha rolled her shoulders, ignoring it as best she could, but she felt it weighing heavy on her like a wet blanket. Orly had been outside to smoke three times and she wished she had a habit that would break the tension. Some mind-numbing sex would work but she was too raw where Kane was concerned to even contemplate it.

"Check this out," Orly said, beaming some files to her handheld.

Orly found the information that Sasha was looking for and gave her a digital copy to read. Each time, a von Buren investigation started because of a report of suspicious shipments. Shipments without documentation that were large enough for the port master to notice.

Sasha read the reports again and found that each investigation started forty-eight hours after the port master had made the report. More than enough time to dump whatever had been shipped and direct the investigators to legal-brought goods.

"Orly, can you check ship manifests for me?" she asked, going back to his side. They had three hours until they left for the airport. Kane was keeping his distance and Sasha pushed her marital relationship to the back of her mind. She needed to focus.

"Sure I can. What am I looking for?" Orly asked. Sasha showed him the report.

"I want to know if von Buren took delivery of duplicate shipments."

Orly scratched the back of his head and read the sections she pointed to. "I'll do the best I can, but as you can tell from these reports, there never was any evidence found to substantiate such shipments."

"Just check." She reread the reports and found that they were always filed by someone identified only as J.B.

"Temple, whose initials are J.B.?"

Temple left the table where he and Charity had been going over maps of Marseilles and the surrounding area. By tapping into a military satellite, they'd been able to get some nice aerial photos of the von Buren house and surroundings. The von Buren place was totally empty in Nice and the house in Marseilles had a skeleton staff.

"When?" he asked.

"From eight years ago up to six months ago," Sasha said. The first report had been back before she'd started investigating Townsend the first time. Before Perry had been taken hostage and killed.

Temple closed his eyes and she waited while he tried to come up with names. If he couldn't find any, she'd run the initials through the STAR list. But she didn't want to do that unless she had to. "It could be Jonathon Burke or Jeanette Basiton."

"Why?" Kane asked, coming over from the corner.

"Well, you have a mole, and someone repeatedly investigated von Buren and found nothing. Von Buren and Townsend are linked through their sons and shared holidays. It could be nothing, but Townsend's main line of business has always been illegal trafficking and von Buren has a legal shipping network in place."

"You're adding two and two and coming up with four, is that it?"

"Yes. Plus, there are inconsistencies in these reports. The investigator didn't check manifests and didn't double-check shipments. It could be sloppy work but HMIA isn't known for that."

"How did you get HMIA reports?" Kane demanded.

"You don't want to know," she said.

Kane started to argue but then she saw him turn aside. Physically make himself take a step back.

Again she realized this wasn't a man on the edge of control. She knew what savage rage did to a person, and allowing them to function rationally wasn't one of the signs. She was beginning to doubt that his career had ever been in jeopardy. He'd been able to talk to his boss and get him to talk to Ano. Something she knew Shubert wouldn't do for just any agent.

"We'll discuss it later. Anyway, Jeanette has been in Sweden working on a drug connection there, so it wouldn't be her."

"Could it be Jon?" Temple asked Sterling.

Sasha kept her mouth closed but glanced over at Orly and saw that he'd made a note of the name. "He works in the director's office. So he'd have access to my file, and he was in the office the day I blew up."

Sasha waited until Temple nodded. The men seemed to have made their decision. She made it for the team. "Then he's our chief suspect for the mole. Orly, see what you can find as far as bank records go. Anything to indicate he's been getting bribes, or that sort of thing."

"I'm on it, boss lady."

"Glad to know I'm not number one any longer," Temple said.

"Me, too, Bruce. I didn't like you in that role."

"Me, neither," he said.

"Sterling, contact Shubert and see if we can set up Burke to pass some information to Townsend."

"What information, Nightshade?" Kane asked.

Sasha thought it over. Everything that she'd taken in along the way of the investigation kind of coalesced in her mind. She knew that Townsend was waiting for them to do something sloppy. It's what she'd do in his position.

"That you and I will be in Toulon tonight and we know where Anna is being held. That you have the list but I'm trying to pry it away from you. And that the only time you'll be alone is by the fountain while I rendezvous with agents from A.R.C."

"You think he'll contact me then?" Kane asked, but she knew that he was thinking out loud and not really questioning her reason. He was giving her the verbal wall she needed to bounce her ideas off.

"Wouldn't you? I think our biggest problem with Townsend is that we keep trying to figure out how he thinks, like it's a different process than we have. But he was trained in the same way we were. Caution is a big part of why he's still a free man."

"You've got a point," Temple said. "In fact, it makes the most sense. If I was Townsend, it's exactly what I'd do."

"The only thing that doesn't make sense to me is if Burke is the mole, why didn't he have Burke get the STAR list?"

Temple glanced at Kane and Kane shook his head. "He doesn't have access."

"But—"

"Leave it alone, Nightshade. I'm sure A.R.C. has its secrets."

She nodded. "We can provide backup at the fountain and have the operatives in place before you get there," Charity said.

"What do you say, Kane?"

"Sounds like a plan. But if anything goes wrong, we're not going to have a second chance to pull this off."

"So we'll make sure nothing goes wrong," Nightshade said with the kind of confidence she wished she really felt.

Le Petit Nice was the kind of hotel that made Sasha wish she was on vacation and not working. But there was no time to linger. While Kane checked into the hotel, Sasha rented a car and met him at the room number he'd sent to her two-way pager.

When she got there, Kane was pacing like a caged tiger. Sasha went to the minibar and found a bottle of Merlot, which she handed to Kane to open.

The mundane chore made him stop his frenetic movements. He opened the wine effortlessly, let it breathe for a moment then poured it into two glasses. He took a small swallow of his drink, watching her.

"What's wrong?" she asked at last. The wine was good but she couldn't enjoy it.

He handed her the note but didn't say anything. Worried, she refused to let it show. Kane's behavior made her fear the worst. Were they too late? Was Anna already dead? Were all their plans for nothing?

She opened the note. She glanced at Kane. He was pale and tight-lipped and Sasha felt him slip a little further from her as she read the words on the paper.

Fox any more of my people and the girl dies.

She didn't know what to say. They weren't taking any more orders from Elias Townsend and the sooner he realized that, the more power Nightshade and her team would have. "We knew he'd be pissed off. This changes nothing," she said.

Kane threw back the rest of his drink and poured himself another glass. "It changes everything. We can't play this game the way you want to. Clearly, interagency cooperation isn't going to deter him."

Sasha went to him and put her hand on his shoulder. He was so tight and tense she thought he might shatter. And then she realized that he was tight because he was fighting against shattering. She didn't know if she could help him put the pieces back together if he did break apart. It had taken her a marriage, a child and two long years to get to the point where she could even think of her own fracturing.

"Trust me on this. It'll work."

He shook his head and pushed her away. Crossing the room to stand in the full sunlight and look out the window at the old prison island of Château d'If. "I can't."

She realized then that Kane thought he was an island. That he didn't understand that islands couldn't really save the day because they were alone and couldn't be a part of anything. Cursing under her breath, she fought against kicking him hard in the stomach to get his attention—really get it this time.

"This is so stupid," Sasha said. "I can't believe we're doing this again. Divide and conquer is the oldest trick in the book."

He pivoted toward her. No emotions shone in his eyes this time. He was the ultimate warrior—cool, aloof and utterly alone. "Why do you care so much about being involved in this? You scarcely even speak to my sister."

He was right. Sasha had kept everyone at arm's length since she'd lost Caroline. That didn't mean she wanted to see Anna die. Especially since the girl meant so much to Sasha's husband. Even her attempt to distance herself from those she cared about had failed. She'd come to recognize that she hadn't really kept anyone out of her heart. Instead, she'd locked them tightly inside, afraid to do anything or feel anything for them. Afraid to hurt, to lose them. "Townsend has meddled in my life one time too many. I'm sick and tired of him being free to do things like this."

"Don't let it be personal, Sasha."

"It has to be, Kane. I think you know that, and that's why you don't want me involved."

"That's not true. It's just…if he takes you, I really will lose control and I don't want to risk it."

"I'll take care of myself."

He sank down on the brightly colored love seat and watched her with tortured eyes. "Come on. Let's go to Toulon and catch Townsend.

"If we don't get him tonight, I'm slipping the leash for good," Kane warned.

"I understand completely." She really did. That didn't mean she planned to let him go.

Twenty minutes later they were in the car heading for Toulon along corniche J. F. Kennedy. Sasha couldn't help but let her thoughts dwell on JFK and the influence he'd had around the world. A strong swell of patriotism filled her and she realized she'd never really be able to go back to the country and be content. She had set a goal for herself long ago, similar to the one Kennedy had set for America to go to the moon. Her goal had been to do her part to make the world a safer place.

And hiding out wasn't helping anyone. Not even her son. He would someday realize his mom was nothing but a big coward unless she started taking control of her life. Confronting her fears.

"Listen, we've been around this," Sasha said. "From now on the stakes will seem higher but they aren't. Anna's life hangs in the balance. You aren't going to give up on her and neither am I. Over the years we've caught a lot of people. We're not going to let Elias Townsend get away." He looked at her. "Ano has put von Buren under house arrest. Shubert has left our meeting time for tonight out where Burke can access it. The plan is in motion."

"What if we're playing into Townsend's hands?"

She'd worried over that very fact. But it was too late to pull up stakes and go home. They needed to follow this through. "Then we'll deal with it."

"Sasha…"

"What?" she asked. If he gave her any more lip, she was tying him to the bed and going after Townsend on her own. She hadn't come this far to end up in a domestic dispute.

"Let's go get him."

"That's more like it."

"Do you have the decoy chip that Orly made?" he asked.

She pulled it from the inner pocket of her vest and flipped in the air toward him. He caught it one-handed and examined it. "It looks just like the real thing."

"Acts like it too, up to a point."

"Let's hope that Townsend buys the act."

Sasha followed him out of the room secretly echoing his hope, but in her heart a new optimism had been born. It felt right to be here. Like she'd trained her entire life for this moment to work with this man on this case. She was the only one who could make a difference and that felt damn good.

Place de la Liberté was a busy square with pedestrians steadily streaming through it. If they hadn't had seven operatives working the square, Sasha would have been worried about Townsend slipping away. But as it was, they were all on and all wired. The night was dark but this area was well lit.

Two houses in the red-light district had been identified as possible hiding places for Anna Sterling. Kane had spoken very little when they'd discussed the houses. He was out in the open waiting for a message from Townsend. Nightshade and Orly would not be part of the Liberté group. They were going to check out the two houses on rue Revel.

"I'm out of here. Orly will continue monitoring your channel."

"Be careful, Nightshade," Kane said in a whisper-soft tone, and she glanced across the courtyard at him. She raised her hand to her lips and blew him a kiss before turning and walking away. She had a feeling in her gut that he was saying goodbye. Which made no sense, but as her dad always said, the gut never lies.

She switched frequencies on her earpiece and put it back in place. Orly was stationed nearby in an old Peugeot. He didn't like the cramped car as well as he liked the Land Rover, but he had to blend in with the neighborhood. And his beat-up car did. "Orly?"

"Right, here, Nightshade."

"Did you put that bug in Kane's piece?" she asked. When they'd left Marseilles, she'd made the decision to put an electronic burr on Kane so that he couldn't disappear the way he had in Café de Paris.

"Yes. I did. Why are you asking, boss lady?"

She shrugged her shoulders to loosen them up under her jean jacket. The holster of her gun rested comfortably in the small of her back. Her khaki pants were loose and were good for using martial arts or running. "No reason, just checking."

"Since when do you not trust me to do what you've asked?" Orly sounded a little ticked off. She didn't really like it when Ano butted into her business.

But that didn't change the fact that something didn't appear right about the situation. "It's just this bad feeling I have."

"Well, don't worry about Kane. I've got him on my screen and he's exactly where he should be."

"Great, which house is first on the list?" she asked. She'd memorized a map earlier. She was entering the Vielle Ville or the old town. It was a maze of streets and shops. She longed for the nice square pattern of New York City or D.C. Life was a lot easier when you could follow a grid.

"The green door halfway down the street on the left," Orly said.

Sasha tried to blend in with the foot traffic in the area called Le Petit Chicago. She saw evidence of restoration in progress, which made for a weird blend of ruined medieval houses and lurid neon signs. She closed her eyes and took a deep breath. Pushed aside the last vestiges of her fear for Kane and worry for Anna. Pushed aside her own feelings of maybe not being ready for this assignment, and reminded herself that she'd taken down Townsend once before.

She was the only agent to ever have captured him. She walked past the building to the end of the block and cut a street over. The back of the building was a tangle of old furniture and Dumpsters.

Next door, a small café had the screen door propped open and the scents of garlic drifted on the evening air. Nightshade made sure that no one was paying attention to the back door. The sous chef smoking on the step didn't even glance her way as she edged through the shadows toward the back of the house.

The back door was locked with an industrial-size padlock. Sasha pulled her lock-pick kit from her back pocket and went to work on the lock.

"I'm in," she said in a soundless voice that carried no farther than her mike.

"Gotcha. I've got a clear view of the front door."

The first floor was deserted but showed signs of recent construction. There were power tools and tables draped with drop cloths. The scent of fresh paint stung her nostrils as she made her way to the stairs. She searched the entire place but found nothing other than signs of reconstruction.

She left via the back door.

"What's next?"

"Two down and one across."

"I'm on it."

"Has everyone checked in?" she asked.

"As of five minutes ago, yes. Want me to check again?"

"Affirmative."

She crossed to the location that Orly had indicated. This place had a light on over the front door and a serious lock on the back door. She had to use her electronic lock pick to get the door open. When she stepped inside, she saw there were no signs of improvements being made, but instead it was a rundown living space. Someone was living here.

"Confirm location."

"Confirming…you're in the right house."

"Everyone check in?"

"Almost everyone."

"Do you still have him?"

"Checking."

She searched the bottom level of the house and

found the remains of lunch and dirty breakfast dishes in the sink. Either four or five days' worth of dishes or enough for two or three people.

She had a foot on the first step when she heard the front door open. Two men were speaking French. She vaulted over the handrail and ducked down behind the stairs, keeping to the shadows.

"Were you followed?" the first man demanded. His voice was low and raspy and oddly familiar. She thought it might be Townsend's.

"No. I took care to make sure that everyone believes I'm a team player," the second man replied. His voice was gravelly and indistinguishable to Nightshade.

She edged closer to the foot of the stairs and peered around the railing but could only see the backs of the men. Townsend was slimmer than Sasha remembered. But otherwise he was the same. The second man was a little over six feet tall and solidly built. He wore an expensive-looking dinner jacket and dress pants.

"Good. Then everything is in place?" Townsend asked.

"Maybe. Where's the girl?" the second man asked.

Townsend moved away from the second man, his cane marking his steps across the hardwood floor. Sasha peered around the edge again. "Don't be impatient. One thing at a time."

"Without her, I walk," the second man said. There was something very familiar about his voice.

"You've made it clear from the beginning what your price was."

"Just so we understand each other," the second man said.

Townsend turned and Sasha ducked back out of the line of sight.

"Yes. I left the decoy package for them to find. It will take them a few days to figure out that it's worthless."

A dim bulb flickered on and the men walked farther into the room. Sasha gasped. The man standing with Townsend was Jonathon Burke.

Chapter 17

Go to the truth beyond the mind. Love is the bridge.

—Stephen Levine

Nightshade backed closer to the wall, waiting for the men to finish their conversation, her mind racing with scenarios and backup plans. There was no backup plan that would work. Dammit, she should have listened to Kane.

Now her husband was walking into a trap. One she'd set up for him. Why had Shubert let Burke go? Was HMIA running their one independent operation and letting A.R.C. provide the cover?

She pulled her gun from the holster. "Burke is here."

There was no response from Orly and she waited another second before trying again. She wasn't concerned for her partner. She knew he was monitoring more than one frequency and watching the street. He'd contact her when he could. But she had to try one more time. "Orly?"

Nothing but silence. Dammit, she was on her own. She took a deep breath and knew that she was well trained and this was the kind of situation that she really excelled at. She'd wait until she had an opening and make her move. She'd beaten Townsend once before, she'd damn well do it again.

She couldn't let either man leave yet, she didn't know where Anna was being kept. She wished she'd had more time to search the entire house before Townsend had shown up. They hadn't called out to anyone, so she assumed that Anna and whoever Townsend had guarding her weren't here.

"No more screwups like what happened with von Buren," Townsend said.

The light illuminated off Burke's blond hair, revealing eyes that were too close together. He probably had some martial arts training and he was younger and seemed more muscled than Townsend. "That wasn't my fault."

Sasha searched her memory for any information on Burke. She knew only that he'd been put on desk duty because something had gone wrong on one of his cases. She should have done more research on him. Shoulda, woulda, coulda, she thought. Her dad always said regrets weren't worth the energy. She knew he was right.

She didn't have more information on this man but as soon as she could, she'd contact Orly again and try to get him to find something she could use on Burke. They were waiting for something to happen.

"I don't want excuses," Townsend said.

From her own dealings with Townsend, she knew that people who made mistakes didn't live long around him. While she wouldn't shed a tear if a traitor was killed, she didn't want to witness one of Townsend's execution-style murders.

"You didn't exactly ask for something easy."

"I just asked for my money's worth. Were you able to get the list?"

"No, I wasn't. But I *was* able to divert the attention from you to von Buren."

Townsend nodded. "I'd rather you hadn't. He's important to my operation."

"I thought this mess with Sterling was your key out of the old business."

Townsend turned on Burke, grabbing the other man by the neck and squeezing. Burke tried to shrink back from him, but could only flail around trying to breathe. "Don't think. I'm not paying you to do that. Just follow orders."

Townsend pushed Burke away. "Yes, sir," Burke said. A bead of sweat formed on his temple and rolled down the side of his face.

Townsend paced around the room. Sasha pulled her gun, waiting for him to present a target. Burke went to the sink and filled a cup with tap water. He swallowed it quickly.

"How'd you find this place?" Burke asked.

"My son did. This was his idea."

"What was the idea?"

"To follow in von Buren's footsteps. Have a legitimate business running concurrently with our other activities."

"So, is he running this operation now?"

"No, he's dead."

"I'm sorry."

"Don't be. The one responsible will pay."

"You know who killed him?" Burke said. Sasha knew that Burke was aware of her identity. She'd talked to him when Ano had conferenced them in with Shubert on the phone. Why had Burke been left in place once he'd been recognized as a traitor?

"Yes. An operative from A.R.C."

"Nightshade," Burke guessed. Then paused, listening. "Someone's coming."

"Get away from the window," Townsend said, and Burke eased back, pulling his weapon from under his coat.

"Sterling's missing." Orly's voice in her ear.

Sasha dropped her arms and moved farther back into the shadows. Dividing her attention between keeping an eye on Townsend and listening to Orly. "Dammit. Did anyone get a visual?" she whispered.

"No, he blended into the crowd and they lost him."

"Our bug?"

"Still blinking but I show him in the square."

Which meant Kane had removed it. "Target is at my location. I haven't had time to search the second floor."

"Gotcha. We'll take care of it."

"Two armed men with Townsend. Permission to take them out."

"Checking."

Before Burke could respond, there was a knock at the door. Townsend pulled a .9 mm handgun from under his coat and gestured for Burke to open the door. Burke hurried to do what Townsend ordered.

One man was pushed through the door and two thugs with guns followed him in. *Kane.* Dear God, what had gone wrong? She edged farther away from the men.

Sasha stayed to the shadows, tensely waiting to see what would happen next. She couldn't take out that many armed men by herself and she wasn't sure what Kane's plan might be. Simply waiting wasn't her style. He knew she was searching the houses on this street. She wished there were some way to let him know she was here without letting Townsend know.

"I've found Sterling."

"Does he need backup?"

"I've got it for now."

"Gotcha."

She redirected her attention to the scene playing out just a few feet away.

"Sterling, I'm disappointed in you. After all our talks I thought you understood what I was offering you was a future," Townsend announced in that grandiose way of his. He moved closer to Kane. Sterling stood his ground and stepped away from the two men holding their handguns pointed at him.

"Aren't we a bit past this?" Sterling said, gesturing to Mutt and Jeff.

Townsend shrugged. "Burke suggested you might have changed your mind."

"I'm still interested in the deal," Kane said. "What is Burke doing here? And why didn't you tell me he worked for you?"

"He's here because I asked him to come," Townsend said with a shrug.

"Shubert knows he's yours. He was probably followed here," Kane warned.

"I wasn't. I know how to evade tails, Sterling," Burke shot back.

"That's why you're pushing papers instead of working in the field." Kane's barb hit its mark. Burke clenched his hands into fists.

"I'm in the office because Shubert was afraid I'd make him look bad."

"You're in the office because you made yourself look bad by being incompetent," Kane retorted.

"Enough!" Townsend broke in on the snarling confrontation. "Burke's competency had nothing to do with why you are here. Did you bring it?"

"Yes."

Townsend lifted both eyebrows and looked at Kane. "I'm waiting to see proof that Anna's still alive."

"She is."

"I'd like to take your word for it but you know how that goes."

Sasha wondered if she should make her move. But still didn't like the odds. She suspected Kane was going to keep talking until he had a clue to where Anna was being kept. Clearly he wasn't armed, but Kane was an expert martial artist, so she wasn't worried about that.

"Were you followed?" Townsend asked the men who had escorted Kane.

"I don't think so. Things were just as Burke said they'd be."

"Good job. One of you take the back door and the other watch this one just in case."

"Yes, sir," said both men in unison.

Nightshade crept quietly through the house until she was in the hallway leading to the back door. She waited until the thug opened the back door and then stepped through it right on his heels. He spun and pulled her around in front of him, wrapping his arm around her neck.

She elbowed him in the stomach, but he didn't even flinch, just grabbed her wrist with his hand. Sasha swung her free hand up and grasped her aggressor's left hand, applying pressure between the thumb and forefinger.

At the same time, she stepped back with her right foot and bent forward, pulling him off balance. She moved her own body forward and down while sending her elbow into his solar plexus again. This time she made a solid connection. While the man tried to regroup, she turned her right leg behind her opponent's left leg and shoved his left arm over his head in a locking position, forcing him down on his knees.

Before he could react, Sasha pulled a zip cord from her back pocket and bound his wrists together behind his back. She pushed him off the stoop and into the bushes. Once he was well out of sight, she bound his feet and used a scarf she found in the pocket of her jacket to gag him.

"Garbage by the back door," she said into her mike.

"Gotcha," came Orly's reply.

Stepping back inside, she closed the door and eased her way back toward the stairs where she could keep an eye on Kane. They were all still standing off in a tense triangle. None of the men trusted the others in the room. Sasha knew that Kane could probably take down at least one of them, but if the man came back in, the odds would no longer be in their favor.

"I thought we understood each other, Sterling," Townsend said.

Sasha debated going out front and taking care of the other guard. But the foot traffic was steady on this street and her actions would draw attention to them.

"What makes you think we don't?" Sterling said.

Townsend drew back his hand and slapped Kane across the face.

"Don't try to be smart."

"I'm not. I want my sister back. You know that."

"Burke here tells me you've been working with another agency."

Kane shrugged. "You know I would be dead now if I didn't at least make it look like I'm cooperating with them."

"We don't have trust between us, Sterling. I need the list."

"I've got it. I'm just waiting to see my sister, which is what we were supposed to be arranging tonight."

"We will, but I'm going to need you to take care of one other matter for me," Townsend told him. "Something to convince me of your loyalty."

"What's that?"

"Eliminate Nightshade."

She saw Kane stiffen with surprise.

"That's not as easy as you might think."

"I know that she's your wife. I know all about her…and the state of your marriage. So you have a choice, Sterling, your estranged wife or your sister."

Sasha held her breath waiting to see what Kane would do.

She started to reveal herself but thought of her son. Could he survive without her?

"Why drag Nightshade into this?" Sterling asked. He'd moved around so that he was no longer between Burke and Townsend. Watching his body language carefully, she holstered her gun and prepared to join in the fray.

"She's always been in this," Townsend said. He held his gun loosely in his hand.

Nightshade watched the three men and ran different scenarios through her head, figuring out whom she'd fire at first and how she'd go after the other man. Though Kane wasn't armed, he wasn't defenseless.

"You knew she was my wife when you contacted

me?" Sterling asked. Nightshade was surprised that Townsend had learned of her identity. Few people outside of A.R.C. were aware of it. She was willing to bet that even Shubert didn't realize she was Kane's wife.

"I recognized her photo from your desk when Townsend showed me a surveillance picture of Nightshade," Burke said. The man was beginning to get on her nerves. She thought about taking out her gun and just shooting him but decided he wasn't worth Anna's or Kane's lives.

"Burke passed the information on to me. Your name kept coming up and I decided to contact you."

"Why do you want Nightshade?" Sterling asked.

Townsend tipped his head down and took a deep breath. "She killed my son."

There was such raw pain in his voice that for a moment Nightshade felt sympathy for him. He had killed many people, some that were close to her. But he wasn't a monster. Something inside him loved his son. Yet, inside him was also something that could justify those deaths he'd dealt.

"Live by the sword, die by the sword," Kane said softly. It was a philosophy they'd once discussed. Being an agent and being in a relationship with one made them have to face death.

"Ironic that you might do the same." Townsend looked up and gone was the grieving father. In his place was the man who'd gone from being one of England's elite warriors to the criminal mastermind he was today.

Kane wasn't intimidated. Burke had backed away from Townsend. Nightshade decided she'd take Burke out first. Townsend was a consummate professional, unlike Burke who'd been in trouble and was unpredictable in the way he'd respond.

"I'm not baiting you, the life you lead, the one your son led. You had to consider the possibility." Kane kept his hands where Townsend could see them, but Nightshade noticed that he moved carefully, as though testing the boundaries of his balance and getting ready to strike.

"You have a son, don't you, Sterling? Do you think you'd be forgiving if I killed him?"

Sasha had her gun in her hand before she realized what she'd done. Aiming right at Townsend, she figured she could take him out before he could give an order that would threaten her son. Her heart beat so frantically that she was afraid it would give away her position.

"No. I'd rip you apart with my bare hands," Kane said. He'd be stepping on her heels the entire time.

"That's how I feel."

Again Nightshade felt a stirring of sympathy. She couldn't recall the face of Townsend's son. The faces of the men and women she'd killed over the years haunted her sleep but she never could really remember who they were. Their names sometimes—most of the time they remained unknown to her.

"My son, however, is a child," Kane said. "If he followed in my footsteps, I'd definitely consider the possibility that he might die."

"As you've faced your own mortality."

"Indeed." Kane smiled at that thought. Lately, everything had been balanced on the razor's edge. She knew he'd thought more about death recently than he ever had before.

Some cases were like that, where you just knew in your gut this time you might not make it back. And you asked the tough questions. Was your life worth the case? This time Kane had answered yes.

"I like you, Sterling. I see a lot of myself in you."

Townsend's words rang true and Nightshade thought she saw a lot of the agent he must have been before bitterness had taken control of his life. He would have made a good bureau chief because he understood the basic philosophies that all agents lived by. But he'd made a different choice.

"A part of me is flattered. You were one of the most brilliant agents to ever belong to HMIA."

She thought Kane might be playing up to Townsend to get him to ease up that ever-watchful stare. Then realized that Kane had spoken from the gut. He did kind of idolize what Townsend had at one time represented.

"But that other part of you has a harder time accepting me for what I am."

Kane nodded. "I do."

"Orly, why was Burke taken out of the field?" she asked quietly, watching the other man move around behind Kane. She wasn't sure if he was going to get another drink of water or if he was setting up to shoot Kane in the back.

"Checking, Nightshade. Charity and Justice are entering the premises from the rooftop. Temple is at the back door. Don't take him out when he joins you."

"Gotcha."

"Enough of the mutual admiration," Burke said. "Sterling owes us something or I'm going to make the call to terminate the girl's life."

Townsend lifted his gun and fired point-blank at Burke. The other man was dead instantly and fell to the floor. "He annoys me."

Nightshade realized they were dealing with a madman. Who in all likelihood was going to kill Kane, Anna and, unless she was very lucky—her.

Chapter 18

Nothing happens to any man which he is not
formed by nature to bear.

—Marcus Aurelius

Nightshade held her gun at the ready, stepping around
the stairs so she had a straight shot at Townsend.
Damn, this wasn't what she'd expected. Was Anna
even in this house, or was she at another location?

She dropped back away from the men and spoke
in a tone that wouldn't carry. "Has the package been
found?"

"Negative. Still searching. Temple took out the
trash."

"Okay. Burke's dead."

"I assumed as much. There's a black Mercedes that keeps circling the block. I'm running the plates."

"Gotcha."

Nightshade glanced back over at Sterling and Townsend. She hated being on the sidelines like this. Hated letting Kane deal with a man that she wanted to take care of. Yet, she knew that she was better here in the shadows. It was where she really did her best work.

Kane watched Burke drop with the cool dispassion of a trained agent. The man who'd been sent to the front door ran into the room with a semiautomatic handgun drawn. He swept the room looking for intruders. Finally holding his gun on Kane.

"Thank you, Pierre, but you're not needed. Where is Jack?"

Everyone turned toward the back door and Sasha felt as if they were staring right at her. She knew she was hidden by the shadows. "I should not have trusted Burke to make sure he wasn't followed."

"Were you followed, Pierre?" Townsend asked, glancing at the other man.

"No, sir. We did everything you told us to. Checking for familiar faces, speeding up around corners, moving through the crowd. I'm sure we weren't tailed back here."

While the thug was talking, Sasha checked in with Orly.

"Is Temple back from trash detail?"

"Negative."

Sasha eased toward the door ready to slip through it.

"Very good, Pierre. Please go check on Jack."

Pierre hesitated and Nightshade realized that he knew that Townsend could very easily shoot him in the back. "Go on. I need you."

Pierre nodded and stalked away. He walked straight past her position without noticing her, and right out the door. Nightshade followed him swiftly. "Jack, where are you?" the thug said.

Deliberately, Nightshade stepped right into his line of fire. He pivoted toward her, raising his gun. She stepped toward him, grabbed his wrist right above where the meat of his thumb and wrist came together. Her hand didn't make it all the way around his large wrist.

But she used force to push his hand down. He punched her with his left hand, hitting her in the cheek. She hit him with a roundhouse kick to the gut. He snarled some curse words at her.

She didn't loosen her grip on his gun hand. Finally, she was able to grab the gun by the barrel and pull it from his grasp. He jerked his arm away as she snagged his weapon. He came at her with a front snap kick aimed at her chin. She twisted to the left, he hit her shoulder instead. It ached.

She'd had enough of this guy. Coming around behind him, she knocked him on the head with her gun hand. He grunted but didn't fall down. She grabbed his meaty neck and felt around for his carotid artery, hoping to put him out the way she had the other guy.

Pierre elbowed her in the gut and turned on her.

He gripped her neck with both hands, lifting her off her feet and closing his hands. She struggled for each breath she drew.

Lifting both of her feet against his chest, she pushed back with all her might and he tightened his hands for a minute before her leverage gave her the advantage and she broke free. He fell backward and so did she, landing on her ass with a jarring impact.

She stood quickly. Bringing the heel of her foot down on one of his hands and twisting the other one behind his back, she forced him to roll over and then bound his wrists and feet. "Number two waiting for you."

"Gotcha. You okay? You sound winded."

"A few bumps and bruises but nothing to write home about."

"Gotcha."

She took a handkerchief from his pocket and stuffed it in his mouth so he couldn't call out a warning to Townsend, before she went back to the door and eased it open. Townsend was concentrating on Sterling.

"Do you have the chip?" Townsend asked.

"Not on me."

Where was he keeping it? She hadn't found it in his home or in his luggage, which she'd searched twice. Nightshade moved back behind the stairwell. She still had a nice clean line to Townsend if she needed it. But until he told them where Anna was, she couldn't kill him.

Kane seemed to be debating the same thing.

Nightshade saw his eyes move from the rickety ladder-back chair to Townsend and back again.

"Tomorrow, be on the 9:30 a.m. cable car to the top of Mount Faron," Townsend told Kane. "Pierre will meet you for the chip. If it checks out, then I will send your sister up on the next car."

"I want proof that she's alive or you're not getting the chip."

"That's my offer, Sterling. Take it or leave it."

"Leave it," Nightshade said, stepping from the shadows and leveling her gun at Townsend.

Townsend fired at Sterling. In slow motion, Sasha saw Kane roll to his side. But not before being struck in the top of his thigh. She heard him groan as he hit the ground. Kane landed a few feet from Burke, whose lifeless eyes stared at the ceiling.

Townsend turned toward her and she had a spilt second to react before she raised the Glock and fired, hitting Townsend in the right shoulder. He stumbled, and staggered back.

Kane lashed out with his legs, trying to trip Townsend, but the older man wouldn't go down. He kicked Kane in his injured thigh, standing over him with his gun pointed right at Kane's head.

Fear and rage battled inside her. This was her nightmare. This was why she'd hidden herself in Leeds. This was the kind of situation where she was afraid to trust. Her gut screamed *just shoot him!* But he was the only one alive who knew the location of Anna Sterling.

"I believe we are at a stalemate," Townsend said in that damn aloof tone of his. It was the same tone he'd used when he'd shot Burke.

"What makes you think that?" Sasha said. "I just heard you order Kane to kill me. Why should I care about his life?"

"But he never agreed. So what's it going to be, Nightshade? Save the man who might kill you to save his sister? Or trust your heart and hope the man who left you won't kill you?"

Townsend's words made sense to a dark part of her. The insecure part that wasn't sure they'd ever had any kind of marriage. But the fact that he was making her debate this angered her. Kane wasn't going to kill her. She knew him well enough to know that.

Skimming her eyes downward, she saw Kane watch her with a combination of anger and something much softer, caring. She realized he wouldn't say anything. He'd said goodbye to her earlier. He'd sacrifice his life if it meant saving his sister's or hers.

Sasha lifted her gaze, meeting Townsend's eyes. Knowing that every one of her fears was broadcast on her face. Her greatest strength and weakness combined. This was it—the moment that would make or break her. She wasn't playing into Townsend's hands anymore.

She'd beat Townsend at his game before, and she damn well could do it again.

The scar on her thigh seemed to pulse as if agreeing that this time Townsend was going down and staying there.

Leaning down, he clocked Kane in the head and she watched Sterling's eyes roll back. The two of them faced each other again.

"*You* were always the one I wanted."

"I had no idea you cared. I would've been happy to bring you in."

"Ah, but I'm not planning on letting you."

"Enough of this. Where is Anna Sterling?" Nightshade demanded. She was Nightshade now, not a bit of Sasha was left. This man was all that stood between herself and life. She knew that despite the way he was watching her, he'd kill her if he had to—anything to make his escape. Because as much as he might want to see HMIA lose face, he prized his own freedom more.

"I see no advantage in telling you," he said, feinting to the left then attacking her from the right with a sharp kick aimed at her gun arm.

Nightshade tucked her body and dropped to the floor, rolling out of striking distance. Hopping to her feet, she lashed out at Townsend with a solid back kick that hit him in the arm she'd injured. But her aim was off and she missed hitting his wound the way she would have liked to.

He spun around with a front kick that connected solidly with her ribs. Before she could recover, he linked his hands together and swung both fists at her head.

She leaned back but he connected with her jaw. Stars danced in her eyes. She leaned toward him and brought her head up, connecting solidly with his jaw.

He groaned and staggered back. He came back attacking her head again.

Damn, she hated getting smacked in the face. This time she diverted the blow with her left hand. Then pushed her right hand in his face to distract him. She stepped forward with a circular motion and pulled his right hand back, trying to force him down by applying pressure just under his elbow.

Townsend twisted out from her grasp and rolled to his feet. He lashed out with a front-hook kick. She ducked but he hit her shoulder and knocked her down. She hit the hardwood floor on the same hip she had the last time. The bruise ached.

She scissor kicked Townsend's legs out from under him. Climbing to her feet, she faltered backward and raised the gun. She wasn't going fifteen rounds with this guy. He raised his gun too.

They faced each other, eye meeting eye, and she knew that if she blinked or flinched she'd be dead before she took another breath. Everything slowed down. She felt that calm that comes before the storm and she took a small half breath and pulled the trigger.

She saw surprise register in Townsend's eyes before he fell to the floor. She hurried to his side, kicking the gun out of his reach. She'd deliberately tried to only incapacitate Townsend, to slow him down. Nightshade had enough dead bodies from the past to deal with.

Leaning over him, she put her gun to his temple. "Where is the girl?"

"I'd rather die than tell you."

"Would you rather your wife die?" Nightshade demanded.

"What? Dora has nothing to do with this."

"If you can bring family members into this, so can I."

"No agency would agree to such a thing."

"You keep thinking you know me, Townsend. But I'm not part of a government group. I'm a renegade with a renegade boss and we'll stop at nothing."

The front door burst open before she could fire. She kept her gun trained on Townsend the entire time. But lowered her weapon when she realized the newest person in the room was holding Anna Sterling with a loaded gun under her chin.

Sasha never broke her concentration. The man who held Anna was familiar to her but she couldn't place the face. He was a young man, maybe in his late twenties. He had dark blond hair and bright green eyes. He held his handgun with a confidence that said he knew how to use it.

"We've got a new player, Orly."

"The Mercedes stopped circling. I'm running his picture through our databases. Team is moving in."

The man tightened his grip on Anna. "Negative. The hostage is in peril."

Her sister-in-law looked more like a kid than Sasha ever remembered. Seeing those scared eyes that were so much like Dylan's cut straight to her heart.

"Things are going ape-shit out there. There are men crawling up the sides of the building," Otto gasped.

"Thank you, Otto. Give me the gun and I'll take it from here," Townsend said, pushing himself to his feet. Blood seeped from the wound in his side.

"Otto von Buren is the second man," Sasha told Orly.

"Gotcha. Team is prepared to back you up."

Anna was blinking furiously and glancing around as much as the gun at her neck would let her. Sasha realized they had a third team member who was ready to do whatever she had to.

"Sasha? What are you doing here?" Anna sounded dazed. Sasha hated the fact that Anna was here now. That they hadn't been able to keep her safe.

"She's a spy like your brother. A liar and a murderer." Townsend walked over to Anna. Leaning down so that his face was level with hers. "She's been lying to you all this time about who and what she is."

Anna's eyes widened. Townsend had rattled her even more than the situation was already doing. Sasha couldn't deny Townsend's charges that she was a spy. "I've never lied to you, Anna. I'm here to rescue you."

"Where's Kane?" she asked. "He said Kane was coming for me."

"Your brother is there," Townsend said, gesturing to Kane's prone figure. Sasha watched her husband and saw that he was controlling his breathing to the extent that his chest wasn't rising and falling at all. There was a pool of blood on the floor next to him. He looked the worse for wear.

"Kane?" Anna asked, her voice papery thin.

Sasha took a gamble. One that she wouldn't have just a few days earlier because it meant depending on someone whose skills she wasn't sure of. Taking a deep breath, she said, "I don't know. He might be dead."

Praying her gamble would pay off and Anna might give them the distraction they'd need to shift the balance of power in the room. Maybe if the girl was distraught with grief or anger, she'd forget to be afraid and just react. Sasha prepared herself to act when Anna did…if Anna did.

"Enough talking," Townsend said.

"Oh, my God, you killed him!" Anna started freaking out and yelling. "You said he would be okay. You said he'd work for you and you'd let me go."

Sasha saw Kane tighten his hands and realized he was going to attack. Everything slowed down again the way it always did when she was about to go into battle. For a moment, Otto was concentrating on Townsend and Townsend on Otto.

"Down, Anna!" she yelled.

Anna dropped like a dead weight and rolled away from the men as Kane came to his feet. Sasha leaped into action, hitting Townsend as he wrenched the gun free of Otto's hands and fired at her. The bullet burned through the top of her thigh. The other one. Dammit, she was going to have matching scars.

She was fatigued and in pain but adrenaline kept the worst of it at bay. She concentrated on Townsend and bringing him down.

Townsend grabbed her shirt, lifting her toward

him. A crazy rage burned in his eyes. Damn, maybe she should have just taken him out before this had gone further. Nightshade grabbed his wrist, holding his hand to her chest. She took her left hand and struck his face with her closed fist. Once her feet were under her again, she regained her balance.

She trapped his arm against her body and twisted around, forcing him downward. Putting her hand on his forehead, she held him steady and restrained him. She took her free hand with a downward knife strike to the groin area.

Townsend gasped and Sasha quickly grabbed both of his hands, bringing them together behind his back. She cuffed him with a zip cord from her pocket and stood ready to help Kane.

Kane had subdued Otto. He had Otto's handgun pointed at the other man. Relief washed over her to see both Anna and Kane alive and safe.

"Well, that didn't exactly go according to plan," Kane said.

She went to his side, standing back to back with him and holding her gun pointed at Townsend. "It wasn't that bad."

"Orly, we're ready for cleanup."

The front door burst open. As one, Sasha and Sterling turned toward the opening and raised their weapons. They were facing local cops with weapons aimed straight back at them.

"Lower your weapons," the officers said.

Sasha started to but Kane wasn't budging. "HMIA—this is a matter for the British government."

"Can we see some ID?"

"You don't need to see any ID," Ano said as she entered the room.

"Chief Mitter will explain everything. Nice work, Nightshade, Sterling."

"Thanks, Ano. Where are the other agents?"

"Temple is watching the back door. Shubert is en route. He and I will personally be making sure that Townsend makes it all the way to the prison cell this time."

"If you don't mind, I'll ride shotgun."

Ano nodded. Kane looked as if he wanted to object, but then he just gave her a look of approval before bundling Anna away. Sasha felt her heart melt at the way he fathered his little sister. She suspected that Anna wouldn't have too many bad moments once she got past her ordeal, because she was surrounded by a well of love. The same love that Kane had been waiting to shower on her.

But that would have to wait a little longer. Nightshade needed closure. Townsend had threatened more than international security, he'd threatened her family, and she needed to make sure he was put behind bars and stayed there.

Chapter 19

Whoever saves one life, it as if he saved the entire world.

—the Talmud

Sasha was back in London one week later, but this trip was a lot different from the first one. She had Dylan with her. He was wide awake and walking around Ano's office. Her father leaned against the desk, Kane was sprawled in a guest chair. Charity, Justice and Temple were all standing against the back wall. And Orly was sitting on the floor building a castle for Dylan to knock down.

Everyone was dressed casually and Sasha for once felt at ease. As if she was exactly where she was supposed to be, surrounded by the people she was meant to have around her.

"Townsend's trial will not be a public one. Since he had been an agent for HMIA, he could be tried by a tribunal," Ano said.

"Shubert was very happy to take him into custody and put him in jail." Kane had been fully reinstated as an agent for HMIA. He had a month's vacation time coming and they planned to spend it in Leeds with Dylan. He had been awarded for his undercover work and would be getting a promotion to deputy director when he returned to work.

"Did Otto ever give up any information to help in the investigation of Hans?" Temple asked. Temple and Kane had sorted out their differences in the gym. They would continue to work together. Temple didn't want to leave the field, so instead of following Kane to the office, he'd be Kane's number-one agent in a new renegade retrieval task force.

"No. He's sticking to his story that he wanted to do something for Paul. One last adventure to avenge Paul's death," Charity said. Something was going on between Charity and Ano. The mother and daughter were acting very strangely. Sasha made a note to ask her friend what was up when they got out of the debriefing.

"Well, that's friendship for you," Justice said, then gave Charity one of her smart-ass smiles. "I know if you were killed, I'd do the same thing."

Charity put her hand over her heart. "Ah, I didn't know you felt that way."

Justice gave her the finger and they all laughed.

Sasha realized that she'd missed more than the action of being in the field. She'd missed the camaraderie of her friends. She'd missed even the postmortem after a case.

"He will have a public trial," Ano added. Otto von Buren was someone they'd overlooked in their investigation because he seemed the least likely to be connected to Townsend and his business. But like Justice had said, the bonds of friendship were strong.

About as strong as the bonds of marriage, Sasha was coming to understand. She and Kane still hadn't talked out the details. But working together and going after Anna had made one thing clear. They belonged with each other.

"Damn right he will. I think Townsend should as well. Then he could get the death penalty."

Sasha shook her head. The sergeant major would never change. He was an Old Testament kind of guy that believed in an eye for an eye. "Dad, it's not your decision."

"Hell, girl, I know that."

"I wanted to commend you all on the job you did. Kane, how's Anna?"

"Back at boarding school with her friends, none the worse for wear. She's made Sasha promise to teach her how to be a spy-girl."

The thought had made Sasha laugh but she'd reluctantly agreed to teach Anna and her friends how to defend themselves. She was going to be showing them the basics of field-operative training for one month this summer.

Her career was still up in the air and she knew that she was the only one who could make the decision that had to be made. Ano had asked her to come back full-time as an active operative. She'd discussed it with Kane but still hadn't felt comfortable confessing her fears or weaknesses. In the end, he'd said he could live with the danger but he couldn't live with a woman who was hiding.

Dylan toddled back to her and she stooped to pick him up, holding him in her arms. This felt right too. She'd proposed to Ano that she train new recruits and work on cases that required her specialty.

"I like the sound of that," Justice said. "Pretty soon, women will rule the world."

"Blimey, Justice, you'd still need us," Orly said.

"Speak for yourself, LaFontaine. I don't need any man."

"You needed me in Toulon."

"Touché."

"Well, I guess that wraps everything up."

Everyone stood to leave. "Nightshade," Ano said. "Can I have a moment of your time?"

"Sure."

"Give me Dylan," Kane said. "I'll wait for you up front."

Everyone filed out of the room, leaving only Ano and Sasha behind.

"Have you thought about my offer?" Ano asked her quietly.

"I've thought of little else," Sasha replied.

"And?"

"I have a counteroffer," Sasha said. "I'd like to return on a part-time basis to fieldwork. But maybe work full-time here in London training new recruits."

Ano leaned back in her leather executive chair. "That might work. When could you start?"

"Two months?" She'd have to arrange for some kind of day care for Dylan and move them to the city.

"Sounds good."

Sasha turned toward the door.

"Nightshade?"

She glanced over her shoulder at her boss.

"I'm glad you made it back."

"Me, too," she said, walking out of the office and down the narrow corridor that she'd never thought she'd be calling home again because she hadn't been able to trust her instincts. Nightshade and Sasha weren't two different women, but two parts that, together, made her whole.

Epilogue

Learn to wish that everything should come to pass exactly as it does.

—Epictetus

The wind shifted to blow from the north but no sound emerged from the surrounding woods. The silence was unnatural. Nightshade tensed, every sense on hyperalert.

Nothing was hidden from her vantage point. In the clearing near the chopper was a puddle of darkness. It could just be shadows from the clouds covering the moon, but she sensed a human presence there.

Townsend. Except she'd taken care of saving her sister-in-law, Anna.

She shut out everything, narrowing her focus to that dark shadow. She waited. The Glock .9 mm automatic felt like a natural extension of her arm. And then he moved, quickly and jerkily. She'd hit him earlier in their exchange of gunfire. She sprang to her feet, a lethal predator sprinting to intercept Townsend.

He pivoted as she approached, leveling his own gun at her. Still in motion, Nightshade leaped in the air and used a forward kick to hit him solidly in the shoulder. A gunshot exploded and she felt the bullet graze her thigh. She cataloged the surface wound and promised herself she'd worry about it later. It wasn't enough to stop her as she brought all her weight down on him. His head bounced against the concrete of the landing pad.

Nightshade twisted her heel in Townsend's shoulder until he cried out and his fingers opened, releasing his weapon. Keeping her gun trained on him, she stooped and picked up his weapon, tucking it into the back of her waistband.

She knelt beside Townsend and pressed the barrel of the Glock against his temple. This time no rage swam through her body. But a calming sense of justice and her ability to separate herself from being just a killing machine.

She keyed the small radio mike attached to her collar and asked for a pickup. She watched Townsend carefully; he was much too quiet to be trusted. She heard the far-off sound of a crying baby.

She scanned the landing pad. A child? The cries grew louder and louder. What the hell?

Sasha sat up in bed. She reached for the pillow next to hers, encountering the warmth of her husband. His eyes opened.

"Okay?"

She glanced at the television baby monitor and saw that Dylan was sleeping soundly. Kane pulled her body closer to his. His mouth coming down on hers. "Yes, I'm fine."

"When the bullets finally ceased, the bodies lay in a coiled embrace on the lifeboat."

The sinking of a cargo ship and the slaughter of its crew seemed a senseless act of violence. But Clea Rice knows the truth and is determined to expose the culprits.

When Jordan Tavistock is asked to steal the indiscreet letters of a friend, he reluctantly obliges, only to be caught red-handed—by another burglar. The burglar is Clea, who is looking for something else entirely.

Only together can Jordan and Clea find the answers to the sinister questions surrounding the sinking of the ship. Answers that some are prepared to kill for to keep buried.

20th April 2007

MIRA

MILLS & BOON
100 YEARS
of pure reading pleasure

100 Reasons to Celebrate

2008 is a very special year as we celebrate Mills and Boon's Centenary.

Each month throughout the year there will be something new and exciting to mark the centenary, so watch for your favourite authors, captivating new stories, special limited edition collections…and more!

FREE!

4 Books
and a surprise gift!

We would like to take this opportunity to thank you for reading this Mills & Boon® book by offering you the chance to take FOUR more specially selected titles from the Intrigue series absolutely FREE! We're also making this offer to introduce you to the benefits of the Mills & Boon® Reader Service™—

* ★ FREE home delivery
* ★ FREE gifts and competitions
* ★ FREE monthly Newsletter
* ★ Exclusive Reader Service offers
* ★ Books available before they're in the shops

Accepting these FREE books and gift places you under no obligation to buy, you may cancel at any time, even after receiving your free shipment. Simply complete your details below and return the entire page to the address below. You don't even need a stamp!

YES! Please send me 4 free Intrigue books and a surprise gift. I understand that unless you hear from me, I will receive 6 superb new titles every month for just £3.10 each, postage and packing free. I am under no obligation to purchase any books and may cancel my subscription at any time. The free books and gift will be mine to keep in any case.

17ZEF

Ms/Mrs/Miss/Mr ....Initials.................................

BLOCK CAPITALS PLEASE

Surname ....

Address ....

....

....Postcode..

Send this whole page to:
UK: FREEPOST CN81, Croydon, CR9 3WZ

Offer valid in UK only and is not available to current Mills & Boon® Reader Service™ subscribers to this series. Overseas and Eire please write for details. We reserve the right to refuse an application and applicants must be aged 18 years or over. Only one application per household. Terms and prices subject to change without notice. Offer expires 28th February 2008. As a result of this application, you may receive offers from Harlequin Mills & Boon and other carefully selected companies. If you would prefer not to share in this opportunity please write to The Data Manager, PO Box 676, Richmond, TW9 1WU.

Mills & Boon® is a registered trademark owned by Harlequin Mills & Boon Limited.
The Mills & Boon® Reader Service™ is being used as a trademark.